ISBN: 1-943924-43-1
ISBN-13: 978-1-943924-43-1
LCC: 2019930649

Chapter 1

Trumpery is defined as something that is attractive but has little value or use. It is further defined as practices or beliefs of superficial appeal but provides little or no real worth. Trumpery now establishes the cause and effect of what was once a great nation.

Trumpery surrounded me in every action on every street from every mouth of every day. Trumpery filled the air from booth to mouth as flowery words spilled to describe the shit each vendor sold. Every trader is more skilled than the last at hawking rubbish as something that without, their consumer could not exist. Tell them the same lie three times, and they will buy anything you shovel at them. Trumpery to sell trumpery.

Trumpery makes even the keenest of minds blind to its divisiveness and trickery. That single statement, having multitudes of application to the remade nation, paves the way of my path to recovery from their conditioning. The illusions fell away into the nothingness of our leader's empty promises and bloated self-image. My thoughts and ideas were becoming my own again, but survival required I acquiesced to the strike laws and moral code of the New Republic.

One hint of defiance, one utterance of disagreement, one look of doubt and even your own mother might turn you over to the Enforcers for justice. The citizens would do anything to gain themselves favor and currency. In this year twenty-one sixty-nine, one hundred fifty years into the rule of our Lord Chancellor Dampnut, trumpery has become doctrine.

MacKenzie Dillon, the name I was given when indoctrinated into the service of the Protectorate, is the only name I remember. I have served the religious zealots since first becoming an enforcer of the law. These laws are the Edicts of the New Republic. I have lived and served the Protectorate for decades thanks to the miracles of science, medicine and the spoils of Space Force.

Everything is privatized, owned by the few, with little left for the masses except the darker trades. Black markets, sex workers, drugs, those exist but are run by conglomerates who are little more than thugs and gangs. Those criminals reported back to the actual criminals, the wealthy members of the Elite Caste. Holo-images of their wares displayed along the back alleys, while the main streets were patrolled by the likes of my team of Enforcers and me.

The Enforcers are the third level of the caste system, just above the General Population and Merchant Castes. Enforcers work as the military and policing body in the perpetual state of martial law. This is the day my journey to thinking for myself again started.

***

I stopped at a booth selling refurbished and upgraded old tech. Personal computer tablets and what used to be handheld communication devices littered the old man's counter. Junk for the most part; nobody used these devices in the upper castes. Even the general population had access to better technology, though they had no genuine need for such luxuries. There were a few items of note, items of which I was not familiar with at the time, but a scuffle nearby pulled my attention away. I noticed the vendor remove some items as I departed.

A fight had broken out at a food vendor. Though there was plenty of government provided nutritional supplements and water, enterprising grunts found a market for roasted rat and in this case what was likely a small dog. Not many options existed for fresh meat from a domestic supply after the 'Unifying Event'. The devastation outside the safety of our Eastern wall meant poison and disease to wild animals and domesticated herds. Any meat imported was well out of reach to the lower castes unless they spent an un-augmented lifetime's worth of credits on a single steak. Even then there was no telling what the meat truly was.

The disaster left the entire globe in a mess. The European Union nearly collapsed. Civil wars over resources and land spread through countries in the Northern hemisphere. Global trade came to a near halt. And yet the ninety-nine percent of the survivors from the Unifying Event in the then United States still looked up to the powers that kept them in their place. It is easier to look up to the rich and powerful as giants rather than look at them and see they stand on your back.

These giants of industry and wealth are little people who spend their lives standing on the backs of the laborers who build their empires. They have a knack for making themselves richer, always wanting more while caring less and less.

3

I was once practiced at separating and muting the sounds of the 'Grunt' levels from my thoughts. The general population, or Grunts, eked out a living as best they could, rarely leaving the first few stories of any city center. These ground levels rang with a melancholy chorus where shouting and chattering of vendors hawked their wares, blending with moans of the downtrodden and forgotten. Overhead the 'safety' drones hummed, hovered, and moved along, scanning the filth-ridden streets for signs of dissent. I boarded my shuttle and flew on to another city.

As I exited my transport, the stench of oppression filled my nose. The barrage of rotting food and garbage along urine-soaked streets tested my gag reflex to its limit. Covering my mouth with a scarf, I proceeded toward the first of many hovels I would visit, enforcing the Edicts of the New Republic and the religious Protectorate.

A haggard woman, leathery face and sunken eyes belying her actual age, turned against her cheating husband. She lifted her ID implanted wrist to my scanner. Expecting credits for trading in the life of her spouse, she was rightly perplexed when instead I grabbed her by the pussy and shoved her toward my comrades.

"Turn her over to the Protectorate Guard for arrest."

"You spoke out against your husband, woman," I said as she protested. "That is a capital offense and earns you a trip to the work camps." I turned to the husband, his stained and crooked teeth exposed as his lips curved upward. "You broke the sanctity of your vow to this woman-"

"But I didn't," he shouted. "She lies and harbors manly resentment. She is a suffragist."

I raised my brow as I turned to watch the woman being dragged away. Perhaps she was a supporter of the past, a believer in equality and rights for all. Those ways and mindsets were wiped away when the country was made 'great again'. Delusion is not a crime but a sickness that can be conditioned away.

"What are the primary edicts of the New Republic?" I asked the man.

"The Edicts are as fake as the news played on the broadcast screens. This country is bathed in the blood, sweat, and tears of the oppressed. We gorge on the lies fed us and-"

The man's words cut off from the squeezing hand on the back of his neck.

My guard pulled the man off the ground and pushed the groveling man toward a prisoner transport. "What sentence has this Grunt earned, sir?"

As the accused begged for mercy, I turned for my transport and motioned my men to take the man away.

"Harvest him. I'm sure someone in the Elite cast could use a new kidney or some other salvageable part of this filthy Grunt."

Though I choked down the bile and remains of my breakfast at my own words, I would re-eat all of it to stay in my position. The punishment for a failure of duty is casting down. I'd sooner die than be lowered to the likes of the ninety-nine percent of the population.

Everyone worked. Everyone had food, shelter, basic healthcare. What the ninety-nine percent rarely got was decent work, quality food or shelter, adequate healthcare or the longevity treatments, education or a chance at a better life.

One of my patrols took me past an education center for the young children of the lower caste. Education is a stretch for the limited curriculum that was allowed to be taught to the Grunts. They were kept as uneducated as possible to limit ideas or critical thinking.

It serves no purpose to recognize those who have no use for more than what the state provides or to think about what was lost when democracy was abolished. History lessons of times before the formation of the New Republic was not allowed unless rewritten by the Protectorate. All they were to know is what existed within the walls that bordered the country.

An Edict of the Protectorate: Keep the masses from knowing for they haven't the intellect to see the truth. The first of bullshit laws the Protectorate enforces to keep the people from rising up against their oppressors. If one doesn't know they are oppressed, then they are easier to control.

I looked around the sea of filthy-faced morons who filled the markets and trash-strewn streets. Beneath the soot and dirt was white skin. All that remained of the population of this country were those deemed worthy of being worked until death for the betterment of the Elite. All others were banished, imprisoned, or exterminated.

Looking at the Grunts, the overwhelming majority of what remained of the United States population after the Cleansing and Unifying Events, I began to notice more than a sea of faces. Trumpery made them feel that they had all they needed. The truth only comes to some at the end, when they peer past the blinding symbol of false representation and hypocrisy. Just then, as they peel away the layered words to reveal mendacity at the core, does one truly see. More and more of the population was waking up, but it would do no good to revolt—not yet.

My meandering thoughts kept me from my sworn duty. I got back into my transport and headed towards more Trumpery in another over-populated under-serviced city along the Great Wall of Freedom that kept the truth out of the New Republic and kept the Grunts in.

Chapter 2

I went to the next shit-hole along the Great Wall of the New Republic, Old St. Louis, to enact justice upon a couple who dared produced a child. It mattered little that it was difficult to conceive naturally any longer. If the fallout from the devastation of the unifying event did not sterilize, then the chemicals in the fake food and the population control measures ensured no illegal reproduction, most of the time.

The Elite could not conceive at all due to all the altering they've done to stay alive so long. Many an Upper Caste family would pay good credits to steal a child from the Grunts, and raise it as their own.

"Take the child," I instructed my men.

"What of the parents?" asked my second. "The usual?"

The usual meant banishment for many crimes against the

Republic, but some violations were more severe than others. This couple conceived without a license, without supervision, and without advising the Protectorate.

"The female will go to a breeding center."

As I turned to face the man, his eyes reflected my own disgust at what I must order. The same fate awaited this man that befell my own father.

"Harvest him."

I became far too skilled at blocking out the pleading cries of those I sentenced until the infant wailed out. I felt the pain of separation once again in my heart. My conditioning, the walls of blind ignorance that the New Republic built into my mind, began to shatter.

I was that child, squalling for my mother's embrace as the robed men snatched me from the safety of her bosom. I was all of six years of age when the edicts of warding children came to pass. Children are raised by the state and placed in the service of the Republic if deemed worthy. Service meant working to enforce compliance of the masses, earning them the rank of enforcer or even protectorate soldier in the caste system. The unlucky were sent back to the general population, subsidized to keep them alive and healthy enough to slave for the comfort of the Elite Caste, until death graced them with a release.

Self-loathing is my reward for being worthy. This was yet another force against my conditioning. The more I began to stop and honestly see, and question, the more my state altered personality faltered.

Until that day, I forgot I even had a mother. Of course, I knew I came from somewhere, but that absolute certainty of one's own origin, family, was eradicated from my conscious mind. I lived decades within a cell inside my mind, walled off from everything I was before the Protectorate stole me. Brick by brick, I was pulling free of the monster the government made of me. I battled my own will to resurface. The mental conditioning fought against the resurfacing of my past.

I spoke Edicts aloud to my men as we prepared to leave, more to reassure myself.

"Worthy are those who enforce the Edicts, for they live to serve the greatness of the New Republic."

I dreamt of the life I might have had as a boy, before the conditioning, the beatings, the training, the anti-aging treatments. I began to see images, more flashes, of my early childhood.

"We live to serve," my men said.

The New Republic ensures we live and serve as long as they require. Another memory from my youth surged. I watched the blue moon as it reached its zenith. It wasn't figuratively blue as the old tales tell of a second full moon in the same month. It was a waxing gibbous, yet made blue by the haze filling the night sky from the ash and snow that still saturated the air all these years after the 'cleansing' of the Unifying Event.

Another lie of the ruling class. The cleansing was regurgitated double-talk for the devastating losses of life after Yellowstone erupted. Knowledge was kept from the general public, but known to those who remember or are worthy enough of the truth. The result of a man-child's tantrum. Too much mendacity. It was time for the truth, time for a change, time for resistance.

"Wait," I called to the men taking away the child and parents. I could no longer stand my part in this system. "Bring me the child."

I turned away from the mother as the fear in her eyes bore into my soul. What she must have thought I meant for the child's fate reflected in the horror-filled paler that washed down her face. I had a reputation after all, for being ruthless in my enforcing of edict violations. I had a chance now to change that reputation, but I had to be cautious while duplicitous.

"The child will go into the lottery."

I held the child closer and stared into its eyes. Such innocence and wonder at the world around it. I looked over the swaddling to notice streaks of pink and hints of feminine patterns. Having a girl child is even rarer to have a child outside specially monitored procedures in a breeding center.

She would go straight to the Protectorate for rearing and obedience training. Later if she were fortunate, she would be determined infertile and sent back to the Grunt levels to live out her life in servitude. Fertile females went into the gestation programs and passed around for harvesting eggs like a prize hen. I couldn't do that, not again.

"Place the parents and child in my personal transport. I will see them delivered for testing."

I spoke the words before formulating a plan. If only then I knew the path this would force me down. I would still not have changed a thing.

The only benefit I found from the conditioning and obedience instilled in the Enforcers, they do not question the orders of a superior. I was an exception since my mental conditioning broke. I was regaining all my memories, most of which I would gladly discard. Yet I am the sum of my experiences and as such, must take the good with the despicable. Nothing I could do would remake the past, best I could hope was a near miss at redemption. But then my conditioning resurged, bringing back my reprehensible character.

Shouting from beyond a line of Grunts pulled my attention. I passed the child along to another officer to place in the transport while I investigated. I charged toward the people who pulled in together to block my path.

I did not have a full company of soldiers. We were not equipped for civil unrest, so I backed away and turned toward my shuttle. I stopped my departure when something impacted the middle of my back.

I turned back to witness the smirks and faces showing ignorance of the guilty party. My conditioned personality took full control and pulled out my pistol before I could stop what happened. I fired my gun.

A man slouched to the ground at the head of the crowd. His chest sizzled from the eight-inch hole where his heart shriveled and burnt. By the time his face hit the dirt, the group was backing away.

"Anyone else wish to show their displeasure in the life the New Republic provides them?" I asked. "Who threw the mud at the back of your superior?"

This was the first time I saw unity among the Grunts. Shaking heads and dispersal of the crowd was the response I received. We usually had multiple offers of information from the Grunts. A person would make anything up to spin tales that might garner favor or credits. My mind wrestled with what to do next.

"Make them talk," I told my Enforcers.

The beatings were severe for the unlucky citizens that were unable to break away from the crowd. My men were merciless in taking all their hatred and prejudices for the Grunts and focusing it on torture. Open view to those who peered from windows and market stalls, the Enforcers kicked and punched anyone they could catch. Those who ran were unable to break free from stun pistols that short-circuited their nervous systems. Even as the unfortunate souls thrashed on the ground from the spasms, my men descended upon them with brute force.

Only when one of my second in command told me of another gathering in another border city, did I call off my dogs. We left the examples we made of disobedience bleeding in the streets. I then ordered my men to our transports, and we went without regard for the Grunts. Our bloodlust was not quenched, but there was fresh meat to the south.

Chapter 3

Every ground town is like every other. I left my men to crowd control as I walked along the back alleys, avoiding the soot-covered walls. I treaded along bricks and stone packed with the ash and muck of destruction. I imagined my face mirrored the disgust I felt for being forced to patrol the Great Wall. It is nothing compared to the self-loathing I feel when recalling every detail of my actions while under the conditioned control. For each act of concealed mercy I performed while free of conditioning, deplorable acts tipped the scales to an extreme opposite while malleable to the Protectorate.

This visit to Memphis was the first response to whispers of a resistance organizing. Over the last several decades, there were small uprisings and stirrings of the lowest Caste becoming unruly. These situations were dealt with quickly and with absolute resolve. Death.

This latest threat to the New Republic became more virulent and open. Posters of a bloated, wooden puppet in the likeness of our Chancellor Lord Dampnut being controlled by a shadowy hand, were plastered over the walls along the path I strode.

I scanned my surroundings, watching a team of Erasers spray down the walls with chemicals, dissolving the posters, painted graffiti, and grime built up since the last time we walked these streets. An involuntary snort nearly escaped my nose as I recalled the mural that previously resided here.

A morbidly obese man-baby in a soiled diaper, donned with a crown and scepter throwing a fit. It was titled, 'The Mad Lord Damp-Pants wants a wall'. As quickly as it was removed, another soon appeared nearby. The Erasers kept busy keeping these political cartoons from the Chancellor's knowledge. There was no telling how he might retaliate.

"I heard that," one of my men, Lieutenant Nathaniel Walters, said. "It was a good likeness, that portrait."

I glanced at him, refraining from the smirk I felt forming. "Careful lieutenant, you don't want to be heard disparaging the Chancellor Lord Dampnut."

Nathaniel stepped up beside me, leaning in to allow his breath to tickle my ear. "It's funny as fuck, and you know it. Besides, nobody heard, nobody is watching..." his hand glanced mine, sending a shiver across my shoulders.

I stepped away as I watched an Eraser nearby turn his head back to his duty. "Do you forget what happened during The Cleansing?"

"Screw the Edicts, Dillon," Nathaniel whispered. "The Upper Castes do as they want, fuck who they wish. Why are the rules different for them?"

I shook my head at the lieutenant's words. This had to be some sort of test. The Protectorate was always pushing the loyalties and obedience of its agents, looking for ways to reveal deviants and traitors.

"Do as they say, not as they do," I said. "Ours is but to provide for the enforcement of the Edicts without question. Do not test my resolve a second time, Lieutenant. And while on duty you will refer to me as Commander."

Raising his hands in mock surrender, Lt. Nathaniel Walters stepped back and saluted. "As you command, Sir, Commander, Sir!" His wink didn't help quell the fires burning in my gut.

Among the many rounded up and expelled from the New Republic during The Cleansing. These groups were immigrants, anyone with opposing political views, religious affiliations other than those aligned with the New Republic, and anyone deemed 'deviant' which included what was then called the LGBTQ lifestyle.

After the wall went up, anyone found on this side of it, who didn't conform to the values of the Protectorate, was exiled if they were lucky. A quick death would be welcome to what faced them these days. Bile rose in my throat as the thoughts and memories returned.

"You have been found guilty of subversive acts," the robed man said to daddy. "The penalty for not turning over a criminal is banishment."

I tried shaking that memory from resurfacing, but the shadows of my past would not submit to the light of the Protectorates empty promises.

My father was a sympathizer, turned in by his own brother for harboring a known degenerate. A family friend who practiced unlawful religion, being Muslim. While that alone, providing shelter and hiding a subversive, would have only been a reduction in credits at the time, my father compounded his crime by reciting forbidden scripture. He spoke the words of the banned

Amendments of the Constitution of the United States of America.

My mother was taken immediately into custody after my father's body hit the floor. A single shot to the temple from a pulse gun. The electric wave fried his brain, but his remaining organs were clean for harvesting. I never saw my mother again after that day.

The burning ache remained in my chest from being carried away and placed into the warding of the state. Raised and conditioned to serve the Protectorate, which in those early days began as a military for the religious right that took control of what was the legislative and judicial branches of government. Their influence was supported by the executive branch. Over time the Legislative and Judicial branches became the Protectorate while the Executive branch revealed who they always were, the Elite Caste of wealthy and influential families.

The Golden Rule never seems to change. Those with the gold, rule.

Saved from more pain of 'resurgence'—the breakdown of conditioning and return of memories—my attention was drawn to the public broadcast screens. They served as billboards for the New Republic agenda as well as news reporting.

The propaganda machine of trumpery replayed the glory of the New Republic bringing order to the chaos of America after the fall of democracy. On the screen, our bloated and deluded leader took precious moments from his latest vacation to actually do his duty for the people.

I don't recall his words, I never listened to them anymore, like most people. The sound of mendacity and made-up words without connected meaning was only a repeat of how great he found himself making grandiose promises that would never come to pass. It was his last few words about an envoy from the West coming to speak about trade agreements.

When the huge orange slug decided he needed returning to his sunshine and golf, the current Press Secretary took over to make a statement.

"Are you in for the pool," a man said from the nearby gambling kiosk. "I have the best odds in the quadrant." He waved me over and pointed to his stakes displayed. "Wagers for any betting man's tastes."

There were odds from every sporting event, to the outcomes of trials, and how long anyone in the service of the Chancellor would last. Betting on how long a Press Secretary would live was a fool's wager, but something made me place a bet that day. "I'll take a thousand credits on her not lasting the night."

"What?" the bookie said. "She'll last at least a week, that one. She's easy on the eyes and has a great rack!"

"Gone by midnight, capitol time," I repeated my wager and moved my hand over his commerce pad.

Having an ID chip in your neck and wrist was handy as it used the body's nervous system as an array. The downside is that it also meant every drone and sensor in the New Republic could always pinpoint your exact location. Everyone was chipped and tracked at all times.

The man shook his head but accepted my bet with a snort. "The Chancellor, Lord Dampnut wouldn't fire that fine piece of ass without at least a week's worth of pussy grabbing. Your loss, Enforcer pig."

I glared at the man while smirking as the words of the broadcast played from the display. The Press Secretary mentioned the upcoming arrival of an envoy from the 'United States'. Those words brought silence and uncommon attention to the billboard screens.

Of all the words and phrases deemed unlawful and censored by the Protectorate, mentioning the former United States was harshly punished. Though the speaker quickly recovered and named the 'Old Union', the damage was done. She'd have been better off speaking about any of the deadly words including entitlement, abortion, diversity or equality. The only thing worse would have been suggesting that Lord Dampnut had anything less than a one-hundred percent approval rating.

As the broadcast screen cut off the address from the Capitol, replacing it with advertisements and promotions for the various sporting and entertainment events, the betting window became crowded.

I nodded at the bookie, having placed my bet at a one-hundred to one margin. He quickly changed the odds before taking more wagers and gave me a look to melt the lips from my smile.

Press Secretaries never lasted, they took the blame any time Lord Dampnut was caught in a lie or misrepresentation. If he didn't look good at all times, someone else was to blame. I shook my head as I felt a tinge of sorrow for the latest victim. She would be harvested before I could spend part of my winnings.

My moment of triumph at the betting window was short-lived, however, as the nagging ache behind my eyes returned. Mention of the United States triggered my childhood memories again.

So long these memories were buried behind the block implanted by conditioning. The extended years of my service to this deplorable institution made the memories—of what was once democracy and multi-national, multi-cultural, multi-religion, open and free society—punishing and painful. I was an instrument of what my parents fought against happening. How the inevitable came to be, was—at the time—blocked from my recall. Bit by bit, the downfall of the United States of America under the guise of making America 'Great Again', was trickling back into my conscious mind. I was becoming more disgusted with myself each day. They only made America 'Hate Again'.

I soothed the conflagration of confusion in my mind by reciting the Edicts of the Protectorate. Making my purpose have meaning, however delusional at this point in my resurgence, was the only method of remaining sane.

"There was chaos before the dawn, the Lord Chancellor brought us light and order. Speak not against his brilliance." I repeated this and other edicts as I gathered my composure.

I stepped back to the shadow of a nearby awning, catching myself from exposing my altered state of mind. Each atrocious act of seizure and arrest I witnessed at the hand of my squadron, required I recite more edicts to justify their actions and my compliance.

A man was taken away from his home after his closest friend informed on his housing a non-citizen. I spoke the edict, "Let not your neighbor, friend or family be false to your obedience, for they must be redeemed by your tale."

Another of my Enforcers dragged a woman from a men's club. She shouted for her right to drink and socialize as men do. "Let not a woman speak ill of any man; for she is permitted not to think manly thoughts, but to abide by them."

I pulled deeper into the blackness of my hiding place to conceal the struggle in my face that betrayed the battle in my thoughts. As two men were dragged from home they were beaten in the street by neighbors for harboring deviant lust for the other.

My men—all but Nathaniel—allowed the lynching and encouraged the mob. I swallowed the lunch that repeated upon my pallet, drinking it down with the bitter taste of bile and sanctimony. A whisper left my lips as the two homosexual men were bludgeoned until they ceased to move.

"Let not the sexual nature of mankind be tested against the natural order for such depravity is rewarded by death and damnation."

Steps of steel-toed boots and the clatter of clergy belts alerted my sense of self-preservation. I struggled to straighten my posture as I observed a superior officer approaching from the ranks of robed and hooded men dressed in the Protectorate holy robes. I only turned my eyes when met by the iced stare of the high commander and First Prime, Protectorate Commander Jon McCord.

The protesting scream of a young girl turned my head, demanding my attention. She thrashed and fought the rough handling of the robed men as they sedated her. These devout men of the Protectorate Edicts placed her on a flower-covered bed aboard a cart, red staining the front of her gown.

The girl had obtained the time of consent. She would be sent to the highest bidder among the disgusting old men of the Elite. If she received a seed and managed to retain a pregnancy, she would be worth something. If she failed to produce an Elite child, there were far worse fates that awaited.

"Bring forth the blossom of young virgins, for they shall consent upon the richness of man," said the Commander, his hand pushing down on my shoulder. "Do you worry about the procreation of our Elite?"

"I worry for the child should she not bear fruit," I answered without thinking.

Expecting a reprimand, I became more unsettled than had I been accused of violating an edict.

"Worry more that she might germinate from a rotten seed, the furthering of a disease-ridden garden."

The Commander spoke out against the Elite.

Chapter 4

McCord stared into my soul with his penetrating glance until I averted my eyes. I wasn't sure what he expected, so I remained quiet.

"Walk with me," he said.

Odd that it sounded more like a request than an order. I followed McCord just the same. Another test I assumed. I couldn't be sure. I was so fucked in the head that I didn't know my ear from my elbow.

This was my superior and a man who seemed suspiciously empathetic to the way the world has turned on its end. So I felt my mind being upside-down was less critical than wondering why my ass was compressing everything I was experiencing so hard that if I farted...Jericho! I'd take down the Great Wall myself.

We meandered down the back alleys, past all the vendors

toward a seedier part of town where the goings on of the Grunts was less monitored. The air was emptying from the chattering of sales pitches from vendors and filling with moans and groans of the sex and drug trades.

One other noise I found absent was the usual and ever-present hum of drones that monitored the security of the New Republic. Spy drones only for identifying dissidence; safety for the general population was not a concern of the Protectorate.

Ducking past a stack of crates and piles of old paper, we stepped into an old shop. Old was an understatement. The place looked to be a throwback to the pre-Republic days where open commerce and communication was commonplace and legal. There were old style printing machines in the space along with ink, paper, other supplies; everything needed to create propaganda flyers was strewn around the establishment. And all of this was contraband.

McCord stopped me with the rise of a hand. He closed his fingers, sans the index and pointed around the room.

"What do you see here?" he asked me.

We were alone in the room. McCord instructed his entourage to remain outside and on guard.

I scanned the room, my eyes returning to examine my commander with each pass. His eyes remained locked on me, watching me observe both the place and him.

"Speak with honesty you reserve for your thoughts alone," McCord instructed. "When I ask a question I expect the raw and honest answer you would otherwise keep private."

I thought about my answer as long as it appeared the Commander would wait. "I see a center for the illegal manufacture and distribution of fake news."

"Fake is a subjective term used to label something that is not real. Any news is information we must pick out the bias from and parse for ourselves. Do not think so narrowly and look again."

The Commander's expression was unreadable.

"Is that all you see?" McCord asked and pointed toward a back wall.

Books. I saw old paper printed and bound books on shelves covering the entirety of the back wall.

"Subversive texts? Banned material? I thought these were all destroyed?"

I pulled out a volume, dusting off the cover to reveal the title—What Happened?—and I tossed it aside.

"These are not all useful or entirely factual, but within each text are nuggets of the past the current regime would rather be erased from history altogether."

I looked at McCord, searching for any clue as to his intentions, revealing such secrets of state. Every conversation, each testimonial or daily report, every action that was taken in the service of the New Republic is a test of loyalty. The slightest hint of dissension or thought counter to the Edicts of the Protectorate could lead to a charge of treason. McCord must have sensed my doubt and fear of answering.

"This is not a test Dillon. I am not a Protectorate snitch."

"You must forgive my hesitation sir, but that is precisely the line of assurance I would use as a tactic for producing an interrogation from an interview."

"As you should, normally. But I am your superior and have given you permission to speak freely."

Speaking with freedom of thought and ideas was the opposite of the rights granted among the citizens of the New Republic. I spent hours every day hunting down and punishing those who dared such violations. Only the Elite Caste had the intellect to think.

"You must again forgive my hesitation, sir, I am unaccustomed to a superior expecting me to think."

"I am sure that was meant exactly as it was said. I appreciate your expressing your backhanded sarcasm. Now look at that old newspaper on the table and tell me what first comes to your mind."

I looked at the table and read the headline. US President begins rounding up the Muslims, Jews, Spics, and Fags. I was horrified but stalled in sharing my initial thoughts.

"The Cleansing," I mumbled. "This was reported in the news then? And nobody thought to stand against such atrocities?"

"You would be surprised how quickly that the righteous quiet down at the line of hate a few rednecks with tiki-torches can erect at a protest." McCord shook his head. "I remember all too well how split the country was when Dampnut was elected President in the first place. I have spent decades trying to get past my own silence. But things have gotten far too out of hand."

I did not pay close attention to what McCord said at that time. Later, upon reflection, I recalled his first attempts at vetting me.

"I'm sorry sir, but I can't read this," I said.

"Because it is banned?" He asked.

"Because it is making my head hurt and my mind reel with changes I can't explain."

"Change is good."

That was all he said and left me in the room to continue looking through the old materials and books that collected dust among the shelves of illegal content.

I saw a flyer on the table. An innocent piece of paper with ink on it arranged in the shapes of innocuous letters and symbols that alone meant nothing. But like ideas and thoughts, when you arrange letters into words and words into sentences, those letters begin to build structured meaning and power.

The headline read words opposite to the Edicts. Subversive texts stirred the minds of the uneducated and were not legal. They spoke of lies and deceit perpetrated by those who alleged protection from the world. What they were was far worse. They were truths of how the very protectors of their existence made the Grunts pitiful excuse for living what it was, to serve.

Another article called to the turmoil of who I really was. The headline read 'The purge of the Scourge'. The report was a scrubbed edit of what happened to those found in the New Republic after the Great Wall. The prominent group among those persecuted were the LGBTQ community. My community as it were, though I was still a child at that time and no guidance for the feelings the Protectorate eventually beat and conditioned out of me.

The photograph made my throat stick, and I could not swallow. Two men of not more than in their early twenties in age were hanging from a beam. The new wall had a line of people throwing stones at the dying men according to the author.

I read how two more deviants were discovered inside the wall. When they refused to turn themselves over to the Enforcers, death sentences were issued and carried out. The crowd was sparse as there were four other public executions this day, but in attendance was one of the deviants' mothers. It is said this poor woman was first to cast a stone, angered by her son's unfortunate deformity.

Of the decades in service as an Enforcer, I witnessed many such brutal executions, many worse. I never had the stomach to wear the executioner's hood, but that made me no less culpable. I could do nothing, say nothing, stop nothing or face the ax myself. Now that all this was turning back on me, remembering the past and person the New Republic tried to cleanse from me, I had to do something.

I looked back at the flyer I found when first entering the room. The ink smudged on the corner, it was not printed that long ago. The Resistance was actively spreading information about the truth.

Someone called my name, releasing me from my dizzying self-reflection.

I exited the space as my soldiers filed into the backroom. Absentminded to the flyer I still clung to, I nearly stumbled as I bumped into another Enforcer, my second in command. I always forget his name, but familiarity breads potential enemies, so I never cared to know anyone I didn't need to.

"Are you well, First?" He asked.

"I'm fine, just do as you are commanded and mind not your commander's business."

He looked at me and squinted, that always suspicious look that devout Enforces give. It is also a look that envious social climbers wear around those with whom they carry grudges or envy.

Before he could question the material in my hand, I shoved past and through a false door that opened into another room. Hidden in the space was a trove of old electronics, recordings, and video displays. The labels had various titles, but all were stamped with Real News.

Chapter 5

I ordered my men to begin collecting the banned materials from the outer space. Thinking myself alone, I closed the door to the hidden room and started my own search for truth.

Thin plastic cases lined the shelves inside. I took one from the rack to find a round and metal coated disc. Written on the top in hand script of black it read The End of Democracy. I was vaguely educated in the past illusions of the government system. Some of the foreign nations in the world still clung to those failed principals.

I must have been mumbling to myself because I soon realized I wasn't alone.

"The principals of Democracy are not the failure, it is the practice and application that is to blame."

McCord must have been in the room when I sealed the door. I know I locked it from the inside to avoid interruption.

"How does that matter today and here," I asked.

McCord grunted and released a humorless snort. "It certainly hasn't mattered in the New Republic or the former government, that is a certainty. There are many countries that have done better than the former United States."

Just hearing the words the United States sent a shiver along my spine. Always remembering that uttering the censored words can get one killed.

"And what exactly went wrong with...the old Democracy here?"

I couldn't bring myself to say United States aloud. I wasn't yet comfortable with the outcome of McCord's testing of me.

"Politics and politicians. None of it ever served the people. So few politicians were the public servants they should have been."

McCord walked over to the shelves of discs. He thumbed along the spines until he found a particular disc and pulled it free. He repeated his search until he returned to me with a stack of recordings. Pointing to a machine on the table before me, McCord turned on the device and showed me how it worked.

My commander slid a disc into the box, and I must have flinched as the buzzing started because he laughed and patted me on the back.

"I admit these older digital disc machines are a bit noisy and clunky compared to our data chips and streams, but you will find the information...enlightening."

I watched the screen before me light up, and words appear. A title for the recording displayed: The fall of the United States.

"What is this? I can't watch-"

"Just watch these Dillon. I'll see that your men clear up and leave. Find me when you have seen enough."

I watched McCord leave. He paused only a moment as he

exited to give me a look that said more than he dared speak, as my men would have heard. Though his lips turned up only a tinge at the corners, his eyes held a desperate gleam of longing for the past.

As I turned back to the screen, I pressed the button that said Play on the monitor.

News reports played in quick succession. They began with the last election in the Democratic system of the United States. An outcome that both shocked and began dividing the nation. Though I was young and uninitiated to the Protectorate at the time, I had scattered memories of those days. Watching these news reports began to stitch together the fragments of my past that the conditioning had expected to obliterate. I was remembering.

A businessman and pseudo-celebrity sweet-talked and bullshitted his way into office. It was clearing in my mind as though just yesterday the riots and unrest began.

Progress in equality and peace were being stripped by new legislation. Former changes to the laws of the nation were getting reversed while bigotry, hate, violence, and ignorance flowered among the roots of lies being fed by the great orange orator.

The worst thing for a broken nation is a leader who places his ego before the people. The more newsreels I watched, the deeper my unsettled stomach sank.

I recalled the days when the lynching started. Immigrants were pulled from their homes and packed into trucks. Homosexuals went back into the closet for fear of being hunted down and strung up in the middle of the night. The government leaders painted over the further divide between the haves and the have-nots with rhetoric about morals and corruptions of the liberal and democratic minded.

The people of the nation bought every trumpery-coated word even when they could not buy food for their family. The new

President fattened up his flock with empty plates of trumpery, feeding their desperation for change. The change began so subtly and slow that by the time the annihilation came, there was no going back.

I changed the disc, sickened already by what I watched and remembered from my childhood. I needed to remember more, no matter the pain my retching caused as I watched the transition of the United States into what it had become.

Over a century and a half of life, and the human mind is said to drop memories to make way for new. They were all still there, buried deep. I began to wonder if I should leave them choking in the thick layers of filth the New Republic seeded in my head.

I pressed on. The next disc was titled The Great Divide. And as I watched it, replayed my own recollection of the seceding of states. I recalled less and less of the truth being played on the television. Censorship became more prevalent as the New Republic took shape. All truth labeled 'fake news' and replaced with what the President wanted releasing. What could not be covered up was the fact that more than half the country pulled free of the union and the United States was no more.

I was ten years old when the Unifying Event was triggered. Already taken from my family and being warded by the government, I was already ripened for conditioning to the travesties that would follow.

I remembered the concussive wave that knocked me to my ass. The rolling thundering in the air was just the beginning. Soon the skies blackened with dark clouds and then the ash began to fall. Yellowstone exploded. The great supervolcano erupted and devastated most of the country, bringing together the survivors. The government was there fast to support and aide. Some thought they arrived a bit too quickly.

I never thought much at that time of the reports of a flaming object falling from the skies above the national park. Few questioned the immediate and swift assistance our President offered in response. They forgot how he ignored the needs of those affected by disasters in the past.

Survival and finding loved ones, that was all anyone affected could focus upon. The helping hand of a benevolent leader was all they saw. The cost of that benevolence would come due sooner than anyone was prepared.

Watching these events from news recordings was surreal because I remembered them now. My own truths were surfacing and damping down the lies I lived over the last hundred and fifty years. I had seen enough, for now, it was more than my shattered mind could handle. If I could reverse the longevity I was granted to not spend another moment with the truth, I would have done so in those moments of despair. I was an agent of evil.

I pushed the stack of discs aside. As a case fell from the top, I noticed the back of the case had a label etched on it. Property of the Old Union Intelligence Agency. At that time, I had no knowledge of the Old Union, this would come later.

The Old Union did not form officially until well into the new regime of the New Republic. The surviving states and territories of the former western United States banded together and remained separatists from the reformation of the Eastern government.

How had this disc gotten here, I wondered. I opened the cover to find not a disc, but a modern data chip. I pulled the chip free of the case and began to look it over. The label accompanying the chip read: Unifying Event of a Mass Murderer.

A scream from outside prevented me putting the chip in my personal device to check its contents. I pocketed the chip and headed for the door. The information in this room was valuable but deadly. Knowing about its existence placed a target squarely on my forehead. What was McCord playing at by introducing me to this place? He knew what this represented before we arrived.

I would have my chance to ask him about it as he was standing outside the shop when I exited. He said nothing to me, and McCord's expression was telling me, later, as he nudged his head toward my men harassing a family. I know he saw me fidgeting with something in my pocket, but still, he said nothing.

We walked toward my enforcers now circling a middle-aged, un-indoctrinated woman, meaning she was no longer fertile and not in the service of an Elite family. Only those in service to the New Republic or in the Upper Castes lived extended or healthy lives. These lowliest of the citizens were what was once called poor.

They were fed, clothed, had hard jobs and given the barest of medical needs, but anything more was scraps reclaimed from the refuse of the Elite or from the black market. They often worked and died on the wall or in what remained of the mines and refineries of fossil fuels.

The woman was found in possession of black market goods, at least that was the charge. It didn't require being a valid charge. The vast majority of violations were always fabrications or trumped up. There was little opportunity for criminal activity in the New Republic. Only crimes against the Edicts of the Protectorate became severe enough for punishment. This unfortunate woman was in the wrong path of some bored enforcers. And she was of mixed descent.

Chapter 6

One of the enforcers grabbed the woman by the hair and forced her to the ground. As he lifted her hair, exposing the back of her neck, another man held a scanner to her skin. The ID chip implanted beneath transmitted her details. Name, caste rank, job designation, the names of her kin both alive and deceased. Her entire history and lineage scrolled on the Enforcer's device.

"Fallen fruit from a bad seed," the officer said. "Looks like you have some bad blood in the family line there Rosa."

She was of mixed Hispanic descent. This meant her family generations ago was split apart, and those without citizenship were deported while those who remained were designated as wall workers.

The President always said that Mexico would build the wall, and in a way they did. Any migrants who became citizens or their descendants born in the then United States were gathered up and placed in work camps along the new border to begin building a wall separating the states from Mexico. When the country fell to the Unifying Event, those workers and any other migrant descendants of other countries became the labor force to build the new structure. The Great Wall separates the New Republic from the wastelands to the west of the Mississippi River. Once the wall was complete, those same laborers were banished.

"Why aren't you at work on the wall, Grunt?" the enforcer asked. "You shouldn't even be within the city market."

Though she tried to explain her presence, my men would not hear her words. They wanted nothing more than to bully the unfortunate woman. Though a term of slang against the General Public Caste, it became a slight against anyone less-than. This woman was considered less-than not just because she was a member of the General Caste, but because she was of both a mixed race and a female.

My men pushed the woman back and forth between them, calling her names. I think they were trying to speak Spanish slurs but failed miserably. I knew some Spanish, not enough to speak it, but enough to know they were spitting gibberish. The woman likely did not even speak Spanish herself as it was banned long before she was born.

Two undernourished children were hiding behind a cart, flinching at the treatment of their mother. An Enforcer guard came up from behind them and dragged them forward. He held the children by the collars of their worn and tattered shirts.

"What have we here? Are these your children woman? They should be in a training program or shipped to the work camps more like it. Their tainted blood would make them useless to perform real work."

The taunting continued, and both children whimpered but held back from crying. These kids have already learned the habits of the Enforcers. Their handlers were trying to instill fear, thinking it a sign of respect. The Enforcers made habits of these displays as examples to the gathering crowds and onlookers. They wanted both to be seen Enforcing the Edicts and also recognized as big tough men. They were small-minded brutes with moral compasses that only pointed down.

I wanted to intercede, but Commander McCord stopped me with a hand to the chest as I moved forward. With my emotions reeling after the flood of memories coalesced in the forefront of my mind, I was compelled to act. The more I pushed against McCord's restraining arm, the harder he pushed back.

"Now's not the time, my boy," McCord said. He kept his voice low and steady. "You can do little for her now that would not affect your own station in the New Republic. We are at a tipping point as you'll soon come to understand."

McCord pulled his hand back and revealed the flyer and data chip that was in my pocket. His hand was so skilled at lifting them I never knew they were missing. I had been fumbling with them in my pocket to the extent that I must have grown numb to the feeling of movement. That or he was a skilled thief.

Putting the contraband back in my pocket, McCord turned to me. "You are going to remember and see more disturbing things than what happens here in the open streets. You'll have to learn restraint and covert tactics if you are to become part of the Resistance."

I was never one to become surprised or display confusion, but my face must have painted a pretty sight.

McCord furrowed his brow and pulled me aside. "You must not show any emotion. You must not appear to be breaking the edicts.

You must learn to work around them and in secret."

"I really don't-"

McCord interrupted and pushed a small handwritten book entitled, 'New Polari', into my hands.

"Say nothing now, but learn the words and phrases in this book. Observe and then act when you can and only in a manner that does not reveal your duplicity. I chose you for many reasons that will become clear over time. For now, just follow my lead."

I relaxed my face and closed my mouth. I had no words at that moment to express the spinning of ideas and facts versus falsities rattling my thoughts. The brief and minute expression of knowing that McCord gave me with a brow twitch and curled lower lip was inadequate toward easing my turmoil. It was the best I would get at the time.

As we returned our attention to the badgering of Rosa and her children, I could only watch as they separated the woman from her two kids. She would be sent back to the wall, being of no use to the birthing centers at her age. The children would be assessed and placed into programs suitable to their intellect, but not above their foul bloodline.

The collection of children was commonly done in this era, though not illegal, it had fallen out of practice not long after I was graduated to the status of level-one Enforcer. My thirtieth year of age, the day I was indoctrinated into the Protectorate and given long-life.

Long-life was the term associated with the injection of a biologically altered parasite at the base of the skull. This parasite attached itself to the brain and altered the way the body regenerated. This caused the extension of human life by decades or more depending on the person. On occasion, it also deepened personality traits, especially in the early days. That is when the mad leader of the New Republic completely lost his shit.

In the case of my men, some of them became more brutish and heartless, but they remained obedient.

Thoughts of my removal from my own family accompanied the words that slipped from my mouth. Both came without warning.

"Release the children," I said as I stepped free of McCord's reach. "Send the woman back, but I will see to the assignment of the children to proper programs."

I was overreaching my authority, and my men knew this. The problem some would think is that my main personality trait became enhanced by the parasite in my head. I was compassionate beyond what was typical for a Protectorate soldier. Which is to say I didn't kill on the spot.

When the realization of my blunder began to settle from my lips to my head, I had barely registered McCord's order for the men to do as I instructed.

"You've apparently not taken a word I said to heart Dillon. An order like that can only come from a high ranking protectorate commander."

"I apologize for my insubordination Commander. It was an impulse brought on by a returned memory."

McCord again gave me another reassuring expression before motioning the children to be taken to an awaiting transport. He stopped me outside the vehicle.

"Tell me about that memory."

"It's more feeling than memory as it yet resurges from the folds of my subconscious. But I recall the unfair assessments and mismanaged placement. I remember the stinging on my body from the beatings that accompanied both success and failure. I remember being moved from program to program until I was fitted within the Protectorate Enforcers."

"And was that not a good fit?"

"In the end, I suppose. But the suffering and treatment of children is not something that is required today."

"The assessment is much better today than it was over a century ago when you went through the programs," McCord reassured me.

"There is still room for improvement in the processes and appraisals. The treatment, however, remains barbaric. Unfortunately, I haven't the rank to do anything about it."

McCord nodded and pushed me toward the transport full of children. "Perhaps I can help do something about that."

Chapter 7

I was given my promotion to First Protectorate that next day. The rank just below Commander McCord. I later learned that the rise in ranks was both for McCord's protection and my own need for having authority to act for the Resistance in secret. The memories and knowledge I both regained and attained were above my clearance, and McCord would likely be targeted as their source. With rank came knowledge and power. Power could be used for evil deeds as well as good.

"Information is a poison to the mind Dillon, remember that," McCord said. "It can bring about quick death in heavy doses, but if absorbed properly, slowly, that same poison can be turned into a remedy."

That was part of an Edict. Information poisons the mind of the unenlightened. Like all the Edicts of the Protectorate, it was a law contrived to keep ignorance and obedience to the regime. Interpretation is not allowed, but that doesn't stop the masses from discussing them. As a First Protectorate, my new job would be to find and root out dissidence. McCord and I agreed it would be the perfect way for me to locate and communicate with the Resistance.

Before I could go about my duplicitous activities though, I was required to endure the pomp and circumstance of an elevation ceremony.

Anytime someone raises among the top levels of a Caste, they are subjected to an evening of introduction where the official announcement of a rise in status is made, and the newly anointed get paraded around from one pompous ass to another. It is a means of allowing the Elite Caste a reason to be seen and introduced, especially to the leaders of the Protectorate. It is essential to know who is above the laws of the land, and the Elite love their celebrations.

The party I could use, in the very least a heavily poured beverage of the alcohol variety rumored to flow heavily at those events. It was something to which I was looking forward. Stale beer and watered wine were the most the lower Castes and even most ranks below First or Second Protectorate could ever acquire. Black market booze could be found but at heavy costs.

I made my way to the bar, anxiety mounting as the hour of my being presented to Elite society drew nearer. I pictured the face of the man I would be confronted with.

The Vice Chancellor was tasked with presenting the new ranks of those being raised this evening. A task VC Damien Pincer openly hated as much as the people he was required to fraternize among.

The shiver that overcame me as I caught sight of Pincer nearly caused my drink to spill. As much as I wanted to turn my eyes from his pale and pinched up face, morbid desire to stare into the eyes of the devil compelled my gaze to linger. An icy cold ran across the back of my neck as Pincer's eyes turned my direction and locked onto mine. He raised a glass to me and nodded, contempt rolled off his face and drifted on the air between us. Only the scent of a spicy vanilla waft drew away my attention from Hell's embracing stare.

I turned toward the source of that stomach rumbling smell. My vision spun a moment as I gazed upon the most stunning face I had ever laid eyes upon. Enraptured by the scent and sight before me I nearly spilled my drink again. Not so much the hidden desire that welled up in me from my groin, but from the person bringing about long forgotten and beaten down feelings. He was the most handsome man with a familiar face.

"Creepy and fascinating at the same time, am I right?" the man said.

After a moment of awkward silence, I muttered. "I beg your pardon?"

"The VC over there. The man can suck the life right out of a room, and people would be powerless in his presence to stop it."

"I'm afraid I wouldn't know," I said.

Was this another test I wondered, or just an Elite socialite playing me the fool.

"Oh don't worry about sharing your thoughts now, or at least the less dangerous ones."

The look coming from this man heated me so much I thought the ice in my drink would melt and water down my alcohol. I took a rather large sip before trying to say anything. I was both afraid of saying the wrong thing and sounding stupid.

He held out his hand to shake. "Hello, remember me? I'm Nathaniel Walters, and please don't think about telling me the VC doesn't give you the willies. I'm sure his own wife scrubs her skin raw with pumice from the Wastes after he crawls off of her. Could you imagine having to share a bed with that vampire?"

"I'm afraid I couldn't...imagine that is, Nathaniel." Then it struck me. "Aren't you in my battalion?"

He laughed and smiled. "I was, yes. Serving my obligatory days of service as an Elite Caste since I don't have bone spurs like Dampnut."

God almighty those lips.

"Please still call me Nate, all my friends do." His eyes twinkled, or perhaps it was my imagination. "And I have a feeling we are going to become good friends now that I'm no longer in your command. At least not the official way."

Only then as he seductively withdrew his hand from mine had I noticed we were still touching. The homosexuality was beaten out of me as a teen—conditioning. It was coming back with my memories hard. The only thing harder was the bulge growing in my pants. I adjusted my dress jacket, thankful for its mid-thigh length.

"It's a pleasure to see you, Nate."

I couldn't believe how fumbling and awkward I became in Nate's presence. Another long gulp of my drink and I was turning to order another. Having my true personality resurfacing made meeting Nate again feel like the first time.

"Oh, get me one as well barkeep. I'll have whatever my good friend here is having." Nate winked at me and nudged himself closer. "Might I have the pleasure of your full name as well, other than Commander?"

"Dillon, First Protectorate Commander Dillon MacKenzie." I thought that giving my rank and Caste might cool things off a bit from this Adonis, but it had just the opposite effect.

"First Protectorate Commander Dillon MacKenzie, you made the Protectorate sound almost sexy there for a second. Congratulations on the promotion. Coming up in the world since last we met."

My nervousness had to show in my face and posture. I knew homosexuality was banned and punishable by exile or death in most cases. A member of the Elite might be able to get away with what they wish in private but not a Protectorate Commander.

"Relax Commander, you'll find that there are things you can say and tease among friends and not be held accountable, especially as a First among your Caste."

"Please call me Dillon or MacKenzie. If we are going to tempt the gallows before witnesses, you might at least call me by a familiar moniker."

Nate laughed again and looked at the bartender who just shook his head. "You mean the barkeep? You needn't worry about him, bartenders here have a strict listen and nada polaray policy. Besides, he's a friend of Gaga too." He spoke the New Polari.

"Who?"

Another laugh and I felt myself falling into his eyes. Deep pools of blue with a tinge of aqua along the inner retina. I could have leaned over and taken his mouth to mine, but fate assisted in preserving my status, rank, and life in the form of Commander McCord.

"I hope I'm not interrupting anything?" McCord said.

His voice was steady, but his tone said he knew what the temperature in my chest was.

"I see you've met Nate. Good, I was hoping to get the two of you together tonight."

"What?" I asked.

I thought the Commander knew another of my secrets I had not shared with anyone in over a hundred years.

"Nate is a friend with connections you'll be needing." McCord nodded at me.

The Resistance. Nate was connected to those who were fighting the injustice of the New Republic. Double targets on his head, being gay and a resistance sympathizer was definitely a trip to the incinerator.

When a deviant of any kind is sentenced to death their body is destroyed. It didn't matter how precious water or organs were, there was no reclaiming anything from a corpse infested with deviant blood. The religious zealots and wing nuts of the New Republic had very dark-ages beliefs that ushered in the Edicts as well as the Protectorate generations past. But as I was finding out, the rule makers were the most deviant and guilty of rule breakers.

"Dillon, it's nearly time to get recorded and your raised rank. Let's head to our table." McCord motioned us away from the bar.

"It was nice seeing you Nate, perhaps we can talk more later?" I asked.

"Oh, I'm not letting you get away that easily. I already tipped a waiter to switch my seating card. I'm next to you."

Shit! I could feel his hand running up my thigh under the table already.

Chapter 8

As it turned out, Nathaniel was more of a tease with the looks and innuendo rather than risking a touch under the table. Later he admitted to me he wanted to, but figured me jumping up and being at full salute would not go over well during the dessert course.

As the dinner presentation started, the New leader of the Protectorate was introduced, Prime Protectorate Commander Jon McCord. As McCord took the stage, it became clear how he was able to raise my rank to his. I was his replacement. His time with me was grooming to take over for his work. McCord winked at me as he claimed the podium.

After the thanks and acceptance of his new position and duties, McCord made quick work of listing all those among the crowd being honored with a ranking that evening. This was before asking us all to join him on stage to meet and be ranked by the Vice

Chancellor and First Lady, wife to the Chancellor, Lord Dampnut.

As I took my place among the others, I was quickly moved to last in the line. Being singled out as the highest rank receiver that evening aside from McCord meant that I would be given special honor and more extended introduction. I hated being the center of attention, but at least I was distracted from thoughts of Nate.

When the time came sooner than I had expected yet longer than I had hoped, it was my name being heralded from the stage.

"From a commander among the Enforcers to First Protectorate is no small accomplishment," Pincer said. "Some might think such a leap unheard of, if not insurmountably difficult. But these are difficult times, and we need leaders who know how best to serve the New Republic."

Pincer invited me closer. "This young man if only in appearance, has served the New Republic for well over a century and done so with great care and honor."

When Pincer grabbed my hand and pulled me closer for a photo, I could feel an imagined burning heat of an enemy blade in my back. He wore his hatred for anything of the old United States or the people who comprised its citizens. Pincer knew my history now, and I would be watched. That was going to make my work with the resistance a bit troublesome. I was more concerned at the moment about getting away from this bastard.

"Thank you, Vice Chancellor, you honor me with your words and this commendation of rank."

"So few reach the highest rank their origins could afford them, and you are among the few who have done so. Dillon comes to us from meager beginnings, a shining light of hope from the dark days of the old ways before the New Republic. His history will help guide him against what was wrong with the old ways and maintain his alignment to the Edicts of the Protectorate."

I accepted my ranking by turning my back and exposing my neck. The chip implanted in me as a teen, then subsequently upgraded as the technology advanced, held my credentials, status, rank and more. The chip was part of a set that all citizens had, the one in the base of the neck, the other in the right wrist. They worked in concert to allow tracking and security, but mostly as insurance against alterations of ID or hacking the Caste system. In the early days of ID chipping, false identification and currency hacking were commonplace. The latest system was seldom hacked and even then near impossible to achieve any alterations.

As I was released from the clutches of the Vice Chancellor, I shook hands with McCord and watched as he retrieved a pin from a pillow. The officers wore a signage pin of the Protectorate, a badge of honor. Though I suspected the pin was more as I caught the quick hands of McCord slip another pin in my pocket.

The First Lady leaned in to kiss my cheek as she attached the sigil on my lapel. "Congratulations Commander MacKenzie," she said in her accent that remained after all these years. "Your family is very proud, no?"

"I'm afraid my family is lost to me since true childhood, First Lady. I know naught of what became of my mother once I was placed within the system."

The First Lady pulled back from me, a look of sadness and understanding crossed her painted face for a moment. She returned a forced smile when hearing the Vice Chancellor clear his throat.

Without another word, I left the stage and retook my seat to the uneven beat of awkward applause. The audience murmured at the words I spoke before leaving the stage. It would appear that not all my history was known, and was likely not supposed to be understood from the look I got from McCord.

When McCord returned from his duties on stage, dinner was

being set out with the first course.

"You have to be careful what you share Dillon. You should not remember such detail of your past." McCord was not scolding me but cautioned me against a loose tongue.

"I would think that being from an early stage conditioning program, some things are bound to remain ingrained within the mind." Pincer appeared behind McCord. "It is too bad you were never adopted into an Elite family by now, but First Protectorate is the best you might do for yourself, my boy. But I'll be watching your progress, perhaps you can be more." Pincer walked away.

"What the fuck does that mean?" Nate said.

McCord poured some wine and lifted his brow. "It means exactly what he said. He'll be watching you."

"You seem unsurprised," I said. "Has that anything to do with the display of pin swapping I caught on stage?"

"In part, yes. But Nate can explain more another time. Tonight is for celebrating."

"This calls for something a bit harder," Nate said and brushed my thigh as he stood. "Relax Commander, I meant from the bar."

As Nate turned, he nearly ran into the First Lady who hovered behind us. "First Lady, my apologies. I didn't-"

"Not worry young Nathaniel. Please, not to let me keep you from the bar. Is where you go in such hurry, no?"

Nate smiled at her, but I noticed the undertone of annoyance. "My Lady." He bowed and departed.

The First Lady Pornia Dampnut was a striking figure. She managed to maintain a look of a distinguished woman of what was once considered late mid-life before the longevity parasite and other medical means of defying age became available. She was in the neighborhood of two hundred years old but didn't look a day over fifty. She sauntered over to the table and took Nate's seat.

"I really must apologize for my lack of knowing earlier. It was inexcusably insensitive."

"Your words are welcome but unnecessary my lady. You shouldn't be concerned over the inconsequential details of your lessors." I meant part of that, but I couldn't help but feel she should have done due diligence before bringing up details from so long ago. "I see you know Nate, are you friends with his family?"

"Nathaniel? Oh well, I would not call him friend per se. I am acquainted with his family of course as there are so few among Elite that I would not know them all." Her smile was faker than her tits as she spoke. "You must be wary of that Nathaniel though, he gets up to much mischief."

She looked at me then moved her eyes down, crossing my chest and then looking into my lap. I felt as dirty as when I was caught with my first morning-wood. She reached over and adjusted my pin. The Omega symbol crossed by the Protectorate Sword of Justice, it was affixed on a slight angle. She moved it into a perfectly vertical position before patting my chest and letting her hand linger.

"Pin looks good on you, but then I'm sure anything would look good on you...or off."

I wasn't able to respond. I felt it would be more than rude to turn down advances of the wife to the most powerful man on the planet, in his own mind anyway. Then again, accepting them would lead me to death by the hands of the mad Lord Dampnut. It also disgusted me. Lucky that Nate chose that moment to return.

Pornia reached over and placed a hand on McCord's shoulder.

"Hello, Jonny."

She turned her head back to Nate and myself.

"Well, I'll leave you fine men to your festivities. I must be getting back to palace." She stood and turned to let Nate back into his chair. One last pat on my shoulder. "I'll be seeing you again, I'm certain, our Commander MacKenzie Dillon."

I caught Nate's dagger-filled glare and heard him mumble.

"My Commander Dillon, you skanky old hag."

I couldn't help but release a stifled chuckle as I accepted a shot glass filled with whatever Nate brought back from the bar.

"Bottoms up!" Nate said with a wink. He downed his shot before I got mine to my lips. "That horny old bitch is barking up the wrong tree as usual."

As I spit my shot out reflexively, I was joined by McCord in laughter.

McCord pushed his glass over for Nate to fill it with the bourbon bottle he rescued from the bar. "I dare say if you'd been delayed at the bar any longer, you'd have come back to her dry humping our Dillon outright."

I noticed the other people at our table laughing to various degrees in agreement. It was common knowledge that the First Lady was not on intimate terms with her husband, though it rumored he still took to the bed as often as possible. It was just not her he chose. So the lovely and sex-starved Pornia sought out other bedfellows, regularly. And it was rumored she had a high ranking lover among the Protectorate.

"I dare say you are a bit old for her tastes though," Nate said. "No offense, I'm the opposite in my preference of older men." That he said so only I could hear, thankfully. "She likes to break in the younger gentlemen such as myself."

"Have you?"

"Oh God no!" Nate pushed his dessert plate away. "Now you've gone and put me off my pudding."

"Sorry."

Nate winked and smiled at me. I melted.

"You'll have to make it up to me."

"I should be getting back to my apartment. I have an early day tomorrow."

In truth, I wanted nothing more than to take him right there and then, but playful innuendo in the Elite crowd is one thing, a display would not go well.

Nate slipped a card into my pocket. "Tomorrow night, eleven. I'll introduce you to some more of my friends and contacts you'll be wanting."

I bid my goodnights and allowed my hand to linger in Nate's a moment longer than customary. McCord saw but said nothing, though I saw the slight smile.

"Goodnight Commander," McCord said. "I had something dropped by your apartment this evening. You'll be needing it for your date tomorrow as well as other clandestine work."

Chapter 9

Sleep did not come to me well that night as visions marched through my mind of possible outcomes for my future. The dreams chased away any hope of rest. Worst of them was watching Nate hanging from the gallows alongside the wall before being led to the noose myself.

In the span of only a few days my life had changed from one of complacent followers and enforcers of the Edicts to being drafted into the Resistance. I had yet to have any right footing in the fight for change, yet I felt the weight crushing my chest. Panting awake, I found my bedding soaked in the sweat of my terror. My head dripped and puddled fear into my pillow.

Morning ablutions refreshed my exterior, while my insides felt the smut forming from my own impending mendacity. I began counting the lies I would have to start spinning as I counted down the minutes before I faced the day.

After seeing the contents of the box McCord sent me, I envisioned cloak and dagger cliches pulled from the few spy films played in the retro cinema.

The box contained devices and tools for changing my appearance, an implant for covert communications, a scanner and other items I had never before seen. Each piece had a distinct look and feel of foreign technology. Looking at the data chip I found in the rebel library, I knew the contents came from the Old Union out west from the markings.

Twenty minutes that is all that I had left of my safe and straightforward existence. I watched the seconds tick by on the wall clock seeing each as a step closer to my demise. My conditioning broke as the parasite inside me was destroyed by a new immunity. That immunity would not make me impervious to the swift and razor edge of the Protectorate Sword of Justice.

Ten minutes and my coms buzzed. A message came from McCord; he was waiting. I grabbed my breakfast brick and headed for the door. Regretting the sandy texture and bland taste instantly, I grabbed a bottled water to choke down the dry and brittle biscuit. Memories of bacon and eggs, my mother's waffles, running outside to play ball in the sun, all things I had not thought about or remembered in a century and more. If there was a chance that what I was setting out to change could bring back simpler days...I was committed now.

I swallowed the last of my dusty morning meal ration and entered my transport. One of the new perks of my position was an upgraded personal vehicle. Another delivery from McCord that awaited me when I left the banquet the night before. I opted against the private driver though. I couldn't have my activities monitored directly.

Five minutes left on the countdown, and I was in the air flying at quarter speed to the Protectorate Headquarters. As I arrived four minutes later, I was greeted by my entire new command staff and their first officers.

I stepped from the landing platform and smoothed my jacket-front. McCord was there, waiting with an unreadable expression. Stepping up to salute my new Prime Protectorate leader, McCord returned the gesture and then shook my hand.

Some ease settled into my tight shoulders as McCord told me to relax.

"Settle yourself, Commander, you look like you march to the firing squad."

I said nothing, but I forced myself to step a bit lighter and with as much calm as I could muster.

McCord took me through the ranks, introducing me to those I now commanded. Many of the faces I was already familiar with. More than a few men I worked with in the past. When the meet and greet was over, my men dispersed and went about already assigned duties. I followed McCord to our offices.

"You'll find a briefing tablet on your desk. Read it thoroughly and then decide for yourself how to proceed."

"And what is my primary objective?" I asked

McCord smirked and turned to leave. "You wanted control over the children's programs. Now you have it." He turned his head as he left. "Careful instead of broad strokes, paint an easier picture, Dillon. Don't fuck this up."

"Wow," I muttered. "Great pep talk."

After closing my door and taking to my desk. I scanned the briefing.

Standard assignments and lists of potential risks for those placed in various groups, but not all the children would survive their placements. It was up to me now to limit the casualties of the New Republic education and vocation training for future generations.

The Protectorate was callous and indifferent to what happened to the children they placed. The bottom line was workers and soldiers were required to keep the Republic running. If there were accidents or worse, there were always more brats to be taken. This was a general way of thinking that I aimed to eradicate. It was the 'worse' part I feared most. Children who did not take to the conditioning parasite and program either died or were locked inside their own head. The body remained in a vegetative state. Those who became useless to the program were destroyed, dehydrated alive and helpless.

I could only imagine the horror of being reclaimed while being alive and immobile. Every drop of water drained from your body until you became shriveled and a dried up corpse. At what point does one succumb and the life drain away, was unimportant to the Protectorate only the purity of the body as they were reclaimed. That meant no polluting the body with chemicals, and there was a special program to remove the adrenaline produced from the shock and fear caused by the process.

I had my first directive then. I would first put an end to this practice of unjustifiable torture toward children. I only needed to formulate a plan, and that would take time.

As I tried to work through more materials and get a grasp on my new duties as First Protectorate, I became increasingly distracted by thoughts of the Resistance. Fumbling with the data chip in my pocket, I submitted to the urge to read through it.

Everything in my office was connected to the central database and computing systems therefor always being monitored, so I had to use the personal reader McCord left in the box of contraband at my apartment.

Always being watched, continuously recorded and monitored, I had to make sure that my actions were not seen. Using the specially created pin that McCord gave me, I feigned a dusting off of my jacket to run my finger along the sword jewel on the pin. This action activated the cloaking capabilities of the pin. That meant any recording devices in my office could be set in a loop in the next ten seconds.

After setting a repeating gesture of thumbing through pages of tablet data, the loop was established, and I could move freely about my office. I took out the personal chip reader from my inner pocket and inserted the chip. What I began to uncover made the bottom fall out of my stomach.

The rumors of an object falling from the skies over Yellowstone before it erupted were right, but it was worse. A secret order from the President of the United States of America was enacted.

Directive code name Unifying Event was a premeditated and orchestrated mission to bring the country to heel. Every step was scrolling along my screen in horrific detail. From the pre-positioning of the national guard and military troops to the federal relief workers and supplies. Each and every resource needed to provide assistance and order for survivors of a national disaster was set and ready. The only remaining item was the initiation of the catastrophe. A projectile from a military space weapon labeled Dampnut's Hammer.

The bile rose before I could swallow it down. I retched my guts out onto the floor in a futile attempt to reach the garbage pail. The Commander in Chief of the nation used a secret military weapon to create a disaster that not only destroyed over a third of the country, but sent the world into chaos, famine, and volcanic winter. The deaths, the climate changes, the disease, and economic collapse, all of it a master plan of a mad man with a bruised ego and desire to keep his power.

I didn't want this information. It was too much to take in. How could someone in charge of the wellbeing of so many be so completely detached from humanity that Dampnut would contrive such evil against the world? And who else knew about this and allowed it to happen? The President could not have acted alone, he's too inept. And who knows about it now?

McCord knows, he had to. And this data chip came from the Old Union. If they still exist, why not take this to what remains of the United Nations? I had what I needed to bring down the New Republic, but then the gravity of it all hit me.

This can't be all that easy. If McCord knows about this, there has to be something else going on. I tried to think, but my head was spinning as fast as my breathing. The only thing I realized at that moment was I had to get some air.

After cleaning up my vomit as best I could, I sat down at my desk to disengage the looping monitor. I headed to my transport, ignoring the officers who tried to engage my attention. When I managed the clarity to take off, I activated the jamming device McCord informed me was in the shuttle. Of all the notes left me in his box of deceit, McCord failed to communicate just how fucked up this all was going to get.

***

As I flew through the blue-grey skies, I scanned outside the vehicle to see what had become of the world. Where once there were rolling hills and mountains was refineries and mines that polluted the air and emptied the Earth of every last grain or drop of fossil fuel. A wall ran from the border of Canada and what was once Wisconsin all the way down western Illinois, Kentucky,

Tennessee, and Mississippi to the Gulf. This kept out the wastes beyond the New Republic. A place of banishment.

Cities on the Eastern Seaboard were overrun with boats and trollers eking out whatever trade they could from the diminished supply of sea life. The cities themselves, few had kept up with infrastructure and crumbled under the ramshackle structures built atop.

Old New York City was one of few places that thrived, due only to the fact that the wealthy Elite and the Lord Chancellor himself have residence and business to conduct from there. This was the hub of what remained of trade with the few countries that dealt with the New Republic. It was also the starting place where I thought I would eventually need to take down the regime.

After hours of flying around the New Republic borders at hundreds of miles per hour, I needed to get back home and prepare for that late evening. As it turned out, I also had to be in the entertainment district of Old New York for my meeting with Nate and his contacts.

Chapter 10

I didn't recognize myself as I stopped just inside the club where I'd later meet Nate. I checked my disguise in a mirror. A cap over my head grew out a new hairstyle and shade. Some tweaks to the face placed pockmarks and a scar over my right brow. A temporary pigment injector changed my eye color. That hurt like a bitch.

My clothes were ostentatious and something one would see on the runway of a fashion house. Articles that one would never see anyone wearing but the most obnoxious of the Elite. That was my cover. I had to look the part of a grossly wealthy and spoiled Elite who had no care for anyone but themselves. The man looking back at me was precisely the type I detested.

The paradox of Nate being among the Elite Caste and yet drove my sexuality and desire wild didn't help. I had to remind myself he was not like the others. As I entered the club, I soon had reinforcing support for my belief that the man I was so drawn to was not the same as these self-serving ass hats.

My choice of clothing was mild compared to the outrageous apparel and accessories the crowd adorned. Little shocked me about the audacity of the Elite, but here there were open displays of what was considered debauchery in the eyes of the Protectorate. No worry of reprisals or arrest, these people paid for their right to do whatever they wanted. That was the privilege of the Elite Caste. Wealth rules the people who enforce the rules.

I took an open table near the stage. From where I sat the mirror around the walls and columns reflected the entirety of the space. I had a perfect view of all the people of influence partying in the after-hours club. Scantily clad young men and women, even children barely of age were providing companionship to a few of the men in attendance. Drugs and booze flowed freely among the Elite, and even some of the political class enjoyed banned activities. If they knew the First Protectorate was only feet away, would they even care?

I had to weigh my duplicity against their hypocrisy. I felt justified when I thought of the acts committed from the Unifying Event until the current day. These were acts funded by the loose change from the deep pockets of these people's families.

"Drink Sir?"

I nearly shit myself. "What?"

"What's your pleasure? Sir?" the waitress stood there, blank-faced and impatient. She made no eye contact.

I supposed it was some sort of protocol that made the patrons feel some assurance of anonymity.

"I'll have a whiskey, neat." Something I heard in an old holo-film.

"As you wish, sir."

She left without a word but soon returned with my drink, and I continued my scan of the room. Leaving the glass before me, the waitress also slid a small message tablet next to it without indicating the sender.

I heard what went on in these illicit hootch bars and entertainment houses. It was an invitation for some company from another patron. People didn't confront one another. If you were interested or not, a reply was typed and sent to the proposer. I was not interested in what the invitation alluded to. It mattered not who it came from.

As the stage lights went up, I felt a tap on my shoulder. I turned to look up at the most repugnant and deplorable of the Lord Chancellor's advisors.

Drucilla Cordwin slithered her way through the early administration being bounced from one role to another. She would drop from the spotlight and then resurface like a roach that refused to die no matter how much it was sprayed with poison.

Looking at her sagging face and thin body made me wonder what witchcraft kept her among the living. With as much influence she still seemed to sway, I admire that she had never taken to surgery or even a new body altogether.

"You turned down my invite? Do you know who I am?" Drucilla said.

"I am not here for you or any other…My decline to your proposal was not an invitation to debate."

Before Drucilla was able to take a seat, I pushed the chair away with my foot. It was difficult to read her expression beneath the layers of paint and folds in her face. She was every bit a walking corpse out looking to drain the youth from some poor desperate man. I was not up for anything so freakish.

"I suggest you might find another victim."

Her eyes I could read or rather could warm myself from the burning behind her glare.

"Suit yourself, but I never forget a face."

I smiled without warmth and said nothing as I turned from her. I certainly wouldn't soon forget that face either, I thought. She was welcome to remember this face, I wouldn't use it again.

The cabaret show was beginning, and I was thankful to see the back of Drucilla swallowed by the shadows produced from the stage lights. I tried to keep my eyes adjusted to the darkness as I watched for Nate to arrive. I wondered what kept him.

My answer came from the voice that began to croon from the stage. I recognized the timber in Nate's voice and the teasing edge to his annunciation. I did not know the song he sang, but I wasn't so much interested in the words as I was in just hearing his voice. I turned to face the stage and nearly dropped my drink.

More skin than cloth invited my eyes. The costume Nate wore —or lack thereof—produced what I expect was Nate's intention. My groin was throbbing before I could try and clean-up my thoughts.

As his finely chiseled and toned form moved with precision and grace, the light gleamed from the sweat beginning to sheen every exposed ripple in his body. The only thing covered was from low hip to upper thigh, but the shorts clung to every curve leaving near nothing to the imagination. Lit from behind, the harnessed wings of white he wore, made for a beautiful view of an angel and me a horny devil.

Nate looked directly at me and sent me that smile that melts my insides. He knew who I was.

I had to order another drink.

Once his performance ended, and the main show began, Nate changed and joined me at my table.

"Heya handsome," Nate said with a wink. "I've not seen you here before."

"How did you recognize me in this disguise?"

Again that smile. "I'd recognize that strong jawline and inviting lips anywhere."

I blushed.

"And you stick out like a virgin at a chastity auction." Seeing my surprise, Nate confirmed my horror.

Finding out that a bunch of repugnant men continued to outbid and spend credits on the hope of deflowering a child reinforced my commitment to rewrite the rules of the programs. I was in charge now and would make those men and everyone like them pay more than credits.

Nate felt my anger mounting in some way. He placed a hand on mine, drawing my attention to him and calming my ire.

"Worse things are happening, and I'm sure you'll find a way to fix things, but now is not the time."

I eventually agreed and followed Nate to another room beyond the stage. The space was cozy and filled from wall to wall with ample pillows and small tables.

A few groups of people sat around the tables, their outward appearances revealing the variety of Castes they represented.

"Dillon, these are my closest friends and contacts with the Resistance. Everyone, this is Commander Dillon MacKenzie, First Protectorate."

Once I was able to meet and speak with each person in attendance, they calmed at the presence of such a high ranking Protectorate among them.

Of the people I met that day, the major players were the three members of the General Population Caste.

Tinker—a nickname—was a man of about sixty years. He

owned a shop that dealt in repairs and acquisition of tech officially sanctioned by the Protectorate for use by the Grunts. He also managed to acquire other—not so authorized—technology. I recognized him from the markets of ground-level of old Washington DC.

A man who worked the materials trade, Samuel, was able to handle explosives and was an experienced chemist.

The collector of secrets through pillow talk and female persuasiveness was a seductress named Scarlett. She was able to provide a list of all the Elite and Protectorate members who visited her as well as much of their unsavory business dealings.

Then there was the one attendee that I was the only one having the slightest upset over. A kid of maybe thirteen, though his undernourished stature and size made him appear around eight. He was a procurer of needful things as he called them. Whatever I needed he would be able to get. He also lived outside the New Republic borders, proving to me the rumors that the New Republic sold more lies about what existed west of the wall.

So now I had met a second crew that expected me to lead them, except this sorry lot was pitted against the first.

"How am I supposed to work both sides while supporting only the one?" I asked. "There are going to be…challenges."

"We'll figure them out as they come. Beside-"

I held up my hand to stop Nate. A voice sounded from my inner ear. The implanted communication device.

"Dillon, if you are still with Nate at that club, you have about thirty seconds to get the hell out of there," McCord said.

"What are you talking about?"

"A raid. I only just heard about it. Get out now."

"Shit!," I said. "Is there a hidden way out of here?"

"Yes, but what's going on?" Scarlett asked.

"A Raid. Now."

Everyone followed Scarlett out through a trap door with me trailing at the rear.

I pulled Nate back a moment and handed him my apartment key. "I suspect you know where I live."

Nate smiled and nodded. "You pick an odd way to get a boy back to your place, Commander."

I had no time for fun, but my libido responded where my voice didn't. "Just get there and deactivate the signet pin in my bureau drawer. Signal me when it's off."

"What are you doing?"

"I need to do my job, but I can't be recorded being two places at once." After Nate acknowledged my plan, I began to close the trap door as he escaped. "I'll see you back there when I can."

Heading for the backdoor, I began removing my disguise and tossing it into the fireplace. I needed to find a way to be there and not be there until I could be in only one place according to the Protectorate monitoring systems. It would take Nate at least fifteen minutes in the fastest transport to reach my apartment. I was betting his family wealth affording him only the best. And Nate did seem to move fast.

The doors began to vibrate under the banging of Enforcers, causing the patrons and workers alike to start running for the back door. They found the way blocked by the new First Protectorate.

I kept as many people possible from leaving, at least from the back door. Several workers made their way to the side room presumably to escape by the secret exit. My concern was not for them. These people are forced to work in places like this to make any extra credits they could get. I was happy to see the Elite and government officials squirm.

Before long I got my signal that the second pin was disabled, so

I called for Enforcers to head around back.

"First Protectorate?" a low ranking officer said. "We weren't expecting you to be here, Sir."

"Well, it is early in my taking over the office. I wanted to see how my team was performing."

The officer was still surprised by my attendance and stood there gawking at me.

"Go about your work. I'm just here to observe."

I watched the officer quickstep into action and call for others to join him in arresting the customers. As I made my way to the front of the building, I took notice of the faces missing from those being detained and questioned.

Drucilla was absent along with any other Protectorate official. They must have left before the raid began.

"Commander MacKenzie," McCord said. "A word."

I joined McCord outside, away from the rest of the Enforcers. "Thanks for the heads up."

"Ya, well it was a bit close. You seem to have done well to avoid suspicion."

"Barely, though I suspect you had something to do with that?"

"I kept the men up front as long as possible. Once I heard from Nate that your other tracker was disabled, I allowed the men to respond to your call."

I nodded and left McCord to his work. I would question the First Prime later in private about the tip-off to the other officials. I wasn't called to be there, so nobody took notice of my departure. I had a guest back at my apartment with which to…entertain.

Chapter 11

Nate left before I woke the next morning. There was a card on his pillow with a heart drawn on it and his com ID. He hand wrote a message to call him later. No one wrote by hand, except when wanting to add a personal touch. A smile came over me as I pulled the pillow to my face and breathed in his lingering scent.

My moment of bliss was interrupted by a pain on the back of my neck as I rolled over. I felt a bit groggier than usual that morning as if I was waking from a dose of sleeping agent. Thinking it just a result of the amount of whiskey from the night before, I put it out of my mind.

The sound of my alarm brought me up and out of bed. I tripped over myself getting up. The room spun for a few moments while I found my footing. I poked myself in the eye with my toothbrush. I decided against trying to shave with the coordination issues I had. Even dressing was difficult as I fumbled to button my jacket.

"How much did I drink," I said to my reflection.

I had no idea how late it was. It was time to face the day again, but this day would be greeted with a little less dread and a little more purpose. All the new experiences and feelings mixed with memories returning made for a heady blend of needs. The need for Nate, the need for justice, but the greatest need was for answers.

I wouldn't get them wandering my apartment reimagining the previous night with my new...I didn't know what to call Nate. I just wanted to call him. Before I could connect the call, another came in from McCord.

"Commander, I need to see you at my office, as soon as you are able." McCord winked and broke the comlink.

***

McCord's office was several levels above mine. I found him on a balcony that overlooked the city below.

Ninety-seven levels above the waters and filth of what used to be ground, we looked over the railing at the sprawling metropolis that existed atop what was once Washington DC. Platforms, supports, and pedways clogged with carts and vendors, while the airways filled with flying cars and transports. The advancements in technology only continued a pattern of destruction as fumes and exhaust smoke choked the lower levels. Towering structures for the upper ranks to occupy blocked what sunlight made its way through the bleak and grey skies from ever reaching the lowest levels.

Nothing grew below level fifty, and even that was barely useful. Only in the uppermost levels where the sky gardens flourished was their food and oxygen producing growth outside of laboratories and food farms. Fresh food was reserved for the upper castes. I noticed the bowl of fruits on the table nearby, it made my stomach turn with contempt. I wasn't hungry, but I would still savor a taste of fresh and real produce.

McCord had to feel my thoughts if not read them. "You disapprove?" He pointed to the bowl.

What could I say? I only shrugged and took a seat.

"I don't like the way things are either Dillon, that is why I need men like you and Nate. As well as all the others in the service of change. But change does not happen overnight."

He picked up an apple and tossed it to me then slid a steaming cup my direction as well.

I took the offered coffee and took a sip. Fresh, not the dusty old powder made from the pressed and chemically altered leftovers of the Elite Castes. I tried to hide the pleasure I tasted, but the rush of flavor overtook my face. Then I sunk my teeth into the apple. I couldn't remember the taste from early childhood, but I doubt I appreciated the juices flowing down the sides of my mouth back then. It was like eating for the first time.

"Nice eh? I prefer tea myself, but this was all that the suppliers had on hand this morning. It seems a shipment was lost recently. These things do happen." He looked toward the balcony.

"You mean it was stolen?"

"More like re-appropriated for the more deserving. I do what I can without drawing attention to my activities. You will learn to do the same."

"I suppose everything in the black markets is easily found in the refuse of the Elite?"

McCord nodded an acknowledgment. He was redirecting things to the disposal units which was then later retrieved by the rebels.

"You've met young Lucas I hear. He is one of the collectors of things that get misplaced and manages to find a use for them where needed?"

"Yes the kid."

"You disapprove?"

"He's a child, Jon," I said using McCord's first name. "He belongs in a school or out playing. He should be somewhere safe from what will begin as this escalates."

"You will find that we will need all the help we can get. Besides, Lucas can look after himself."

I agreed to disagree, but I understood the need for utilizing whatever talents and resources we could muster.

Our conversation covered the supply chain for the resistance and critical initiatives for gathering intelligence. McCord had been redirecting food and water, tech, small arms, and some transport vehicles. There were also Protectorate Enforcer uniforms and riot gear in the list, but no heavy weapons. Not yet.

"We are not planning an armed rebellion yet, if we plan this right, there will be no need."

"You plan on turning the people against the Chancellor with the truth of his-"

"Transgressions." McCord completed.

"That madman is a mass murderer. I've seen the data chip material."

McCord set his glass down and sat back. "It's not as simple as that, Dillon. Lord Dampnut may have pressed the button, but he is not now nor ever was the brains behind anything. The only thing that fat bastard has ever done is stir people up by talking in circles and shoveling out bullshit."

"So then we take them all down. Do you even know who they are?"

"Some, but again it's not that simple. These people have been controlling things for so long their justifications have become their own moral code. The wealth of the world can buy silence and spin truths into fraudulent claims against their enemies with a call or a bribe. They have a way of always popping up. The shit always surfaces no matter how deep in the muck you try to push them."

"That can mean two things, McCord. It's past time their shit surfaces and we pile it on so thick they can't shake it off. How can you deal with these people knowing what they do? I'd love to kick their asses so hard they have to sneeze to shit."

"I admire your moxie, but we are playing a long game here. Better to seduce the devil and have him whisper in your ear. Secrets collected to add to the pile of trouble we will dump."

"One thing I don't understand," I started. "From where is the financing of the Resistance coming?"

I found out that there were many wealthy and influential contributors to the movement, some domestic but most foreign. I could see where the leaders of other countries wanted to upset the New Republic government; most foreign relationships were lost when the New Republic formed. The land was forced out of the United Nations. Even Russia eventually became disgusted with Lord Dampnut when they realized he double dealt and never kept promises.

The smallest surprise was McCord confirming the origin of the data chip was the Old Union. However I was thrown a loop when McCord admitted that it was given to him personally.

"You'll have a chance to speak with OU agents soon enough. There is an Envoy coming very soon for trade talks."

McCord saw the surprise in my eyes. If we started open trade with the Old Union, then Lord Dampnut would have to reveal the existence of surviving American civilization outside the wall. Later

McCord advised me that there had been trading done in secret with the OU for decades.

"On to the next thing I asked you here to speak about," McCord said. "What are your plans for the children's programs. I need to be prepared for how to help you."

I had to figure out the best way to deal with the Enforcers' brutality first. Unwarranted arrests led to the taking of children. Girls generally ended up in breeding centers while the boys went to work camps if they did not show the capabilities to become Enforcers. Nobody volunteered for the service of the Protectorate. Soldiers had to be drafted. After twenty years service, if they chose, a Protectorate soldier could go back to the general population to become a merchant. If they served for life, they could be given the Long-Life treatment as I had.

"You still have to do your job as First Protectorate. If there is a sudden halt to the activities of the Enforcers or Protectorate Guard, you will be-"

"I know…I'm walking a tightrope that's on fire."

"Spanning a shark-infested ocean," McCord added.

"Thanks."

"I know it's not an easy position, trust me I'm on a tightrope of my own. The trick is to soak your shoes in water first and have a raft ready to catch you when you fall."

I committed to using the contacts I already gained and those I would meet along the way. One such connection was Scarlett.

Scarlett already took two children for me to place with families outside the wall. Her connections became a great asset when trying to move children that were taken. I couldn't bypass them all, and send every child away, but I could make sure the most vulnerable among them was seen after properly. The others would need special care in the placement of programs.

I would also need to rewrite the protocols on how children were trained, treated, and punished. Though not as poorly managed as when I was among the drafted as a youth, there was a history of mistreatment that clung to those who graduated. Those leading the programs were once part of them and thus perpetuated their own experiences back. It was a cycle I intended to break.

Chapter 12

My days became filled with the fielding of reports and deciding to which calls the Enforcers would respond. I selected the most easily interfered with to attend in person. Where the routine calls for public gatherings and demonstrations were left to the Enforcers, I went where I might save lives and best disguise my perfidy.

I received a tip from Scarlett that there was unrest in Old St. Louis over some contraband. This at first made me wonder about why it warranted my attention, but Scarlett insisted I see for myself.

After taking off from my vehicle platform, I climbed quickly to sixty thousand feet and pushed to pursuit speed which against the jet stream put me at around seven hundred miles per hour. Luckily the 'quiet spike' at the cruisers nose allowed for attracting less attention as did my altitude. I was acting in an official capacity, though I intercepted the report before the dispatch received notice.

I arrived at the Wall's Missouri Gate. One of several egress points along the Great Wall of the Republic. In the beginning of the reformation of the US after the supervolcano, this wall was created under the guise of protecting the borders from plague-infected people. This was only to pick at the fear of survivors who readily agreed to abandon those needing help. The primary purpose was for controlling those who remained within the confines of America that hadn't the sense to leave.

The thirty foot high gates were only opened to send out those who would not abide by the changes set forth by the President. By the time Dampnut renamed himself Chancellor and abolished the election process, anyone who posed a threat was already banished to the wastes to the west.

Now that I knew about the Old Union, I wondered how many of those banished since the early days survived versus succumbing to the wastelands. I often wondered if there were outposts or settlements between the Wall and the Sierra Nevada mountains. Taking a survey flight was impossible since all flight computers were programmed to prevent flying outside of the borders without clearance commands from the Protectorate.

As I made my way from my cruiser, I went to where I saw Lucas duck behind a vendor wagon. I hastened my step to reach him without notice from the crowd.

The Wall Watch was on scene and searching the locals for contraband. Scarlett's message said that there was a report of something found among a known black market trader's goods that roused more than the usual harassment from the Watch. She never mentioned Lucas would be present.

"Lucas, what are you doing in Old St. Louis?"

"I come and go from here and a few less known points along the wall, but that's not the point. You got Scarlett's message?"

"Obviously. What then is this thing of interest and who has it?"

Lucas produced an object from beneath his jacket.

The device looked to be a mobile computer of some sort but was only about seven inches long by four and a half an inch thin. It appeared to be non-functional. The back side carried the distinctive mark of the Old Union.

"Looks to be drained of power," Lucas said. "But I've no way to charge it."

A shout from behind alerted me that my presence was noticed. I handed the device back to Lucas.

"Get this to Tinker and tell him to get it working for me."

Lucas nodded and stuffed the unit back in his inner pocket.

"Who's there?" the Wall Watchman said. "Come out here."

I turned toward the husky voice as Lucas disappeared into the shadows. As I turned toward the Watchman, I allowed him to see my insignia and rank bars.

"First Protectorate, Sir. I didn't...I mean, I wasn't-"

I raised my hand to stop the man's stammering. "It's quite alright, watchman. I should have announced my presence when I arrived."

He looked past me, into the alleyway where Lucas escaped into. "Who was that you were speaking to Sir? Was it a suspect?"

"No, just a child I thought might know something." I walked toward the man, turning him to walk with me before he asked more. "He had nothing useful. Now, what have we going on here?"

"Nothing you should have concerned yourself about Sir. I mean the First Protectorate has better things to worry over than some contraband and minor dissidence over nonsense."

The watchman told me about some rumors spreading about outsiders—People not from the Republic—who lived outside the Wall within the Wastes. Technology with English writing but apparently not from NR—meaning New Republic—origin.

"So where is this device?" I asked.

He shrugged. "Rumors. None of the Watch has seen nothin' nor do we expect to. This kinda shit-talk happens on the regular. People ain't happy with nothin' they get around here."

"And what do they get?" I asked. I was rhetorical yet interested in the response.

The Watchman looked at me like I wasn't white. "I'm not sure I understand the question, Sir."

"Never mind," I said seeing that another watchman was dragging a child in from the alley.

It was Lucas.

"Isn't this the boy you were speaking to?"

The Watchman's tone was clear. He glared at me.

"No," I said. I couldn't give up my position. "What is his designation?"

The Watchman grunted his distrust. "He hasn't any. No ID chip."

This was a problem, but one I could get past.

"That is not possible. Did you have your chips removed kid?" I tried to signal Lucas with a look.

Lucas spat at me.

"Well that was rude," I said. "I have just the place to teach you some respect."

I grabbed Lucas and turned to take the device from another watchman that had found it while searching the boy. When he tried to pull it away, I reminded the man of who I was.

"I am taking this boy and anything he had in his possession back to the Protectorate. Your compliance will be noted."

As I walked back toward my transport, Lucas struggled against my grip.

"You are a false friend-"

I gripped harder on the back of Lucas's neck. "Hold your tongue until we are alone."

The Watchmen stood near as I opened my vehicle and placed Lucas in a back seat. I made a show of restraining him and stowing the contraband in a compartment. Before I took my position, I turned to the lead Watchman who still wore an expression of suspicion. Pulling my personal device out of my pocket, I motioned him closer.

"Credits for your diligence." I motioned him to present his wrist chip.

A bribe disguised as a reward has always been effective at blurring the borders where allegiance teeters. One of my most recent returned memories was of one of the last things my father said to me. Never underestimate the power of using human greed as a tool.

The watchmen took the credits, though I didn't see the doubt wash from the lead Watchman thoroughly. I didn't expect it would, but having transferred payment to him, I now had a record of his identity. That information would undoubtedly be useful.

Lucas swore and cussed at me from the back seat as we took off. He refused to quiet down and listen. The only way I got him to silence was accelerating our takeoff and easing up on the inertial dampening system. The g-force shut him up...well, he wasn't talking anymore.

Once we leveled off at cruising altitude, I re-engaged the dampeners and released Lucas's restraints.

Lucas tried to swing at me, but he was too dizzy to hit his mark.

"Settle down already kid. I had to make a show of taking you in."

When he was easing up, I reached into a storage box and

retrieved a chocolate bar to give him.

Lucas took the candy, ate part of it and wrapped the rest up before stowing it in his jacket. "Now what?"

I tilted the OU device around in front of me. "Now we take this little toy to Tinker."

***

Tinker made short work of fixing the device, though he could not activate it. He sat at his desk, mountains of gadgets and parts scattered around him. His workshop was hidden away in a back room of his store. Tinker was a merchant of refurbished tech, items that were allowed by the Protectorate for general public use. Most of it toys and leisure items that played music or received broadcasts from the press corp. The already cramped space was closed in tighter by shelves and racks of more parts and scavenged garbage from the higher Castes' trash.

"It has power, but there is a chip required to connect it to the Old Union network," Tinker said. "I suspect though it might not work completely even if we had a chip."

"Why not?" Lucas asked. He shared his candy bar with a younger child that lurked behind his leg. "Is it too old?"

"Oh it isn't the age of the device, it appears rather modern. I would assume the New Republic frequency jammers might prevent a signal."

"Easy," Lucas said. "We just go outside the wall."

Tinker and Lucas argued over why that wouldn't work. When Tinker said that the device would appear on NR sensors the moment it was turned on and connected, Lucas countered with a trip deep into the Wastes.

"And how do you propose a foray into the wastelands?" I asked.

"It's forbidden without clearance."

Lucas made several suggestions including sneaking onto a mining train, which I dismissed immediately. Besides the environmental hazards, I would never have an unguarded moment to attempt using the device. All miners were also thoroughly searched pre and post excursion.

"You can always bribe the guards," Lucas said.

"And how would I explain possessing the number of credits that would cost?"

While we argued, Tinker was busy talking over secured coms with someone. He ended his conversation and then began rummaging through boxes of parts.

"No need for such a scheme," Tinker said, handing me a small cube. "I just spoke with McCord, and he will arrange a reason for you to fly outside the wall."

I took the cube and looked it over. On one side it had a small opening with three prongs. "What is this then?"

"When you are set to fly out, you need to have this installed just below your command console. It will proxy the clearance codes transmutation and record it. That will allow us to use it again whenever needed."

"But those are one-time use codes," I said.

Tinker winked at me. "You and I know that, but with this little beauty installed, your shuttle won't."

Chapter 13

I left Lucas with Tinker. The old man assured me he would get Lucas a counterfeit ID chip installed so he wouldn't be caught again. I also told Lucas to avoid the Old St. Louis gates for a while.

By the time I arrived back at the Protectorate headquarters, McCord was waiting for me in my office.

"I hope your day was fruitful?" McCord asked.

That was code for did you get what you need?

I nodded the affirmative and took a few moments to freshen up in my office restroom while McCord spoke.

"I mentioned previously that you would be afforded the opportunity to meet someone from the Old Union. That meeting has been scheduled for a short time from now."

By saying 'short time,' McCord's tone meant to get yourself together we were leaving.

I finished cleaning up as best I could and took my dress uniform out of the closet. Meeting a delegate from a foreign nation required all the proper ceremony. Even though this was a meeting with people from the same continent, the Old Union was as foreign to the New Republic as was Canada or Mexico. They were all treated equally as threats to the Republic.

"Stop making yourself all up Dillon," McCord said. "Best to get this over with. State dinners annoy the piss outta me. Particularly those held at that damn space station."

It would be my first visit to the New Republic Space Force Station since my conditioning and subsequent training for the Enforcers. The station was first built in 2120. Many things have changed with the station since then.

I hated that place for different reasons than McCord. People's memories and identities were stripped from them there. Not like mine were in the past, but with worse methods. McCord simply had a disdain for space and artificial gravity.

We walked our way to McCord's platform, McCord decided to fly me to the station. When I suggested we take a Protectorate shuttle, he insisted we take his vehicle; I'd not be needing mine as he suspected the possible unfolding of events that evening.

McCord made arrangements for me to meet the Envoy from the OU and then escort him back to his prearranged transfer station seven hundred miles west of the Republic border. When I argued that they arrived in their own shuttle, McCord advised that it would not be leaving the space dock.

***

The reception hall on level nine was filled with Elite of the highest order. The most wealthy and influential of the upper caste milled about the room, drinking and nibbling on things that never made their way below level seventy. They whispered and nodded, sharing gossip and seeds of information as they each tried to leverage themselves against rivals. No matter how much they had, it was never enough. The powerful and wealthy always craved more of everything like a junkie wanted their drug of choice.

The drug pushers in the capitol were the government officials and the rest of the ruling caste. Those who ran the government had the power, so they thought. The one constant that remained after the Unifying Event, the Elite—the wealthy—were the ones wielding the government with the real power behind the New Republic.

I found myself disappearing among the security forces and then among the outer edges of the reception hall. I needed to distance myself from the stench of the pompous and self-important Elite. As I melted into the shadows behind a pillar, McCord sent me a message to join him at the receiving line. It was time for the Envoy to arrive along with his delegates and our own leaders.

More than one glance of disgust and annoyance was cast my way as I pushed through the guests to join McCord. We waited at the base of the stairs where we were placed before the Elite in meeting the honored guests and our host, the Chancellor himself.

The Vice Chancellor arrived first, accompanied by Drucilla. The woman managed to paint herself up with makeup to look even more revolting than had she been a corpse for weeks. Drucilla also managed to make herself present everywhere there were plays for power and influence. Her expression of absolute confidence must have been fueled by the secrets with which she traded.

The VC and Drucilla met us at the base of the stairs, both smiling at me with all the warmth of the sculpted ice on display behind us. Drucilla's eyes held a hint of recognition as though she knew me.

The moment the realization dawned, I stole Drucilla's smile. Now I had some power, and she had a blank stare.

Drucilla realized it was me in disguise at the nightclub. Whoever tipped her off didn't advise there was a scout sent in before the raid.

The Vice Chancellor pushed Drucilla along, nodding at me and shaking McCord's hand. He was both making room for the next arrivals, and avoiding me, seeing the effect I had on his companion. The VC whispered with Drucilla before giving her a laconic smile. He turned to me with a bit more interest in his eyes.

I looked away as the First Lady was arriving.

Pornia never arrived or left anywhere on the arm of her husband, the Lord Chancellor. She seemed nothing more to him than an old trophy that gathered dust. On occasion, she would be taken out and shown off, but like any trophy collected and forgotten, Pornia held no value to the Lord Chancellor. This explained any ignorance of her extramarital activities.

Pornia lingered far too long with me. "Hello, again Commander MacKenzie. You look quite delicious this evening."

"You flatter me, my lady." I purposely refrained from returning her compliment. There is no point in waving steak before a dog you don't wish to pet.

When the Lord Chancellor began his walk down the staircase, the room erupted in cheers and applause. This greeting was not accolade but compulsory. Another rule to feed the maniacal ego of the mad Lord Dampnut, Chancellor of the New Republic and savior of the old America.

Typically, protocol demanded that Dampnut be last to enter any room so that all attention would be directed toward only him, but there were special circumstances tonight.

Dampnut lingered only a moment with each of us as he passed, looking through every one of his receiving party.

I noticed his eyes. They appeared to hold no life, like a child's doll. I watched him walk with deliberate movements toward the podium as though he followed a programmed course. I assumed he was being medicated as rumors implied he was getting more deranged and erratic.

When he started speaking, the Lord Chancellor lifted away the vail of speculation. The revelation of just how mad the leader of the New Republic was becoming seemed to dissipate. The people whispered for only a moment before settling into acceptance. This was how things were, and that was who he was. Somehow, everyone around me was okay with the man who represented—destroyed—our country being what he was, a crazed puppet. But who was pulling the strings?

I scanned the gathered dilettantes of the various houses. What used to be lobbyists and interest groups in the old democracy of the United States dissolved into piles of waste that the new shit was built upon. Each House or Family in the Oligarchy had their own interests, and those are what they pushed upon the bloated fool who pretended to run the country. Looking at all their white, puffy, over-indulged faces, I saw more than one glint of distaste for the evening's guests. Fewer than a handful of attendees could be seen actually enjoying themselves.

Lord Dampnut shook his head while emitting a gravelly wet rumble that accompanied the wobbling of flesh hanging from his ancient chin and neck. As fully-fleshed the man is, it was hard to believe the fat didn't press out his skin like a ripe melon. To think he allowed himself to remain the same for over a century, paranoid and considering himself the model of male perfection, just added to the mystery of how this egomaniacal, bigoted, sexist, came to rule.

The stories of his original rise to power are laced with myths of a simple-minded breed of human that once roamed freely and hidden amongst the rest of the population. Only when they heard the subliminal words of his speeches. They read the hidden texts in print to emerge from their shells spreading hatred and stupidity in the name of the great orange man-baby. That trumpeter of lies would become the President and then self-appointed Chancellor, Lord Dampnut.

"Okay-okay, I know we are all excited to be here. I know I am," Dampnut said.

His squinting eyes and pursed lips moved back and forth, casting a mindless gaze over the crowd.

"It's been too long since I last favored you all with my presence. I know we had to turn guests away. So, so many wanted to be here with me tonight. Could we have booked a bigger space? Perhaps. But lucky we have the national broadcast so everyone can see me across our Great Nation. Everyone is watching, I'm sure because this is huge—maybe the hugest event ever."

While the marionette spat out words like one of my old-world Pez dispensers, I scanned the audience. They were as dead to the blathering of the Mad Lord as was I. The occasional glance toward the podium was the most attention given our exhausting leader. Looking at him, in his natural state of pontificating his own narrative on the state of reality, Dampnut was without a clue or care that nobody listened. I found an empty table in the corner and took a seat.

I found myself imagining Dampnut's reaction if he realized how worse it was for his words to fall on indifferent rather than deaf ears. My mind created an image of the Chancellor in nothing but a diaper, holding his breath until he turned from orange to deep red then purple. His head growing larger as pressure might build up, forcing his triple-twist comb-over to fall forward into his face. As I prepared for the dreamt up popping of his fat orange head, a hand on my shoulder brought me crashing back to what masqueraded as reality.

"Are you truly enthralled by the circumlocution of that megalomaniac?" Commander McCord asked. "He certainly can talk bullshit. And nobody knows bullshit like him."

I chose not to explain my fantastical imaginings. "What brings you back to my honored table?"

McCord sat down next to me and motioned his chin to the far right of the Chancellor. "Our guest is arriving."

Chapter 14

It was the first time I recalled feeling such duality in the first impression of someone. As I looked at the Envoy from the Old Union, I felt at first hope and sense of possibilities of a better future, until his eyes met mine.

A shudder ran along the hairs on the back of my neck that sent them on edge. I couldn't place the feeling at the time and should have registered the warning. The old saying that hindsight is twenty-twenty makes sense only once you've stepped out of the blurred hope of what you wanted to see, rather than the truth that only experience can clarify.

The Envoy, Eli Minsk, smiled as his eyes moved from mine to McCord's. He walked toward the Lord Chancellor as he was introduced, snapping his attendant into motion behind. The scrawny personal assistant struggled with a large parcel that protruded from both sides as he carried it double armed across his body.

"Our very good friend from the west coast of this great land," The Lord Chancellor started, "has come all this way for many reasons. First, he is going to tell you all about his great, great cities out west and then confirm what we know about the wastelands."

The Envoy stepped forward reaching out to shake hands with the Chancellor. Before their hands could meet the Envoy was pushed to the side as the Chancellor reached past to grasp the package held by the Envoy's assistant.

"I believe you have something for me Minsk," said Lord Dampnut.

As the Chancellor retched the wrapped parcel free of the assistant's hands, he began tearing the wrapping off, throwing it every direction.

I remembered then my childhood and the excitement I once held on Christmas morning. Even as an eager child, I was never as impatient or self-absorbed as the Lord Chancellor was at that moment. Yet I found myself as curious about what was being unwrapped as the others around me. What could possibly hold such desire for a man who could demand anything he fancied any time he wanted?

Even the Vice Chancellor raised a brow of interest.

"Is this what you promised me, Eli?" Asked Dampnut. "I thought it destroyed before the unification."

The Vice Chancellor cleared his throat. "Careful, My Lord."

Dampnut looked up at Damien Pincer, the Vice Chancellor, and grimaced. The moment passed quickly as Dampnut's hand met with the object below the wrappings.

"My star, it's my star from the walk of fame!" Dampnut clutched the star and pulled it to his chest. "I knew it wasn't destroyed. Fake news. I always said it was saved."

"I'm afraid-" Eli started.

"That old sidewalk must be missing this great-great star. Mine is the best star that ever was placed."

The Chancellor began reminiscing about his days long ago when he was a pseudo-celebrity on what was called reality TV.

I held my own memories of the days in which viewers were sucked into watching television shows alleging real people in their daily lives or situations. Of course, they were all produced and altered by editing for ratings. Oddly I do remember the Lord Chancellor being portrayed as a sizable douchebag. I laughed out loud at how there was some truth in those shows of old. A hand on my shoulder shocked me silent.

"I tried to tell him it was a replica," the Envoy said.

Where he came from and why he was next to me I didn't understand at the time. "I beg your pardon, Sir?"

"The star. It's as fake as Dampnut's hair."

I looked back at Dampnut, coveting his prize as the Vice Chancellor's guards ushered the blubbering fool out from the reception hall.

"I don't think it matters," McCord said as he joined us. "Our Lord Chancellor has always had a problem discerning between real and fake, particularly where it comes to news, friends, and breasts."

I watched McCord and the Envoy share a quick look and chuckle. The kind of look that silently spoke of shared agreements and secrets. The examination lasted only a second, but I saw what later I should have seen for something more than an alliance.

"I see you have found our young First Protectorate, Dillon MacKenzie." McCord smiled and motioned us to an empty alcove.

We waited as guests began to filter from the room. With the abrupt departure of the Lord Chancellor, the festivities were halted.

The Vice Chancellor walked the room dismissing the guests. The attendees were now free to leave and wasted no time in finding themselves a better place to continue living up the excess of their privilege.

"Look at them all scatter like locusts," Eli said.

I chuckled.

"What is it, Dillon?" Eli asked.

"I find it appropriate, the comparison to locusts."

"Go on."

"The Elite class, even the lower castes in many respects, will feed off those below and surrounding them. They take their bounty and fill their already fat bellies from the work of others, leaving behind hollowed carcasses reflected in the empty coffers of the lower caste."

"Exactly so my good man," Eli said. "If only the New Republic could see the value in an economically leveled government and society like we have established in the Old Union."

"Interesting," I said.

"What is your thought? I see doubt on your face."

I looked to McCord who nodded I share my thoughts freely.

"You said 'economically leveled', but not equal."

"Well there will always be those who have more than others, it is the nature of man to collect as much as one can when they find something to treasure. We have, however, lessened the gap and heavily tax the more wealthy to supplement those with...lesser prospects."

He chose his words with precision, this Envoy, I thought. What was he not saying and why was he the one chosen to represent the OU?

"If I may, Envoy, why are you here and not the leader of the Old Union?"

"That would be like a mongoose entering a viper pit," Eli said.

"If Penny Seloni were even mentioned in front of that Lord Chancellor of yours, I think his head would explode."

Eli told me of the history between the OU President and Lord Dampnut. She was a political leader back when the Changes were beginning for the United States. She was part of an initial effort to thwart the underhanded dealings of the majority leaders backing President Dampnut.

With each action made by the President, counteractions were put in motion. Leading the charge was Penny Seloni. She stood up against everything he attempted that was in direct violation of the constitution or country to the public approval.

"Of course words were always exchanged between them, and Dampnut took to his chirping account to blast insults at the opposition. I actually miss those times, reading Dampnut's childish rantings. They were quite entertaining if not baseless and full of inaccuracies. His lies were as bad as his grammar."

After hearing about the dynamics between them, it made sense why Seloni did not dare come to the New Republic herself. Besides being a former rival and pot stirrer to Dampnut, she was a she. A woman had a place in the eyes of the New Republic, and it was not among the decision makers or leading parties.

"We even thought of sending our Secretary of State, but the reception committee for the New Republic said that would not be acceptable."

"Why is that?"

"He is Latino, you know, brown. He is from Puerto Rico actually and Dampnut probably still thinks that is part of Mexico. Your Ruler has a problem with skin color besides white."

"Used to be the only color that mattered was green," McCord said.

McCord looked at me as though I missed his joke. "You know

money used to be printed and had green ink."

I looked at him with dumbfounded eyes and exaggerated wow. I remember old money.

Before I could continue, the Vice Chancellor, made his way to our table. Pincer arrived with a security detail.

The Vice Chancellor scanned the three of us, mistrust hid well by his posture but ever-present in his pinched face muscles. The man managed to hold a look of someone who stepped in shit and is forever looking for the source of the stink. Funny how nobody ever realizes the foul stench that offends them is coming from themselves.

"I hope the abrupt end to our festivities has not sullied your impression of our hospitality, Envoy," Pincer said. "But I do feel that it best you depart now that the Lord Chancellor has taken ill. I'm sorry your gift garnered the response it did."

"I believe the response was as expected, Vice Chancellor," Eli said. "It was how the response was received that is in question."

I watched the Vice Chancellor closely, hoping to sense a crack in his icy façade. He held his poise. I had to admire the ability to remain level. But then ease of emotionless response would come quickly to a man with no soul.

"Whatever the expectation, you'll find a tight grip on what is perceived. In any case, Envoy Minsk, I believe it's past time my detail escort you to the terminal. Your pilot has been sent ahead to ready your shuttle."

Chapter 15

Our short walk to the terminal was longer than I hoped. Every step ticked in my head for each second I didn't want to be near this man. The silence swallowed the echoes of our footfalls along the inlaid marble floors. Once the terminal entry gates came into sight, the Envoy's pilot waved us on as he entered the shuttle and finished pre-flight checks.

The moment the concussive wave and flash of flames burst from the shuttle, I had my eyes on the Vice Chancellor. There—in half a breath—I saw a glimmer of something I would later align with satisfaction. A planned effort to keep the Envoy within the New Republic. But surprise and misdirection were the way of the Vice Chancellor, and he was ready.

"Well, that was unexpected." Pincer managed to paint a look of concern over his pale and pinched but smooth-skinned face.

It still unnerved me, seeing a man so aged with the skin of youth but the eyes of a corpse. More advances in medical science and technology from the spoils of Space Force secret missions. The rich and powerful defied age and death, at least those among the highest of the Elite. The government denied the fake news of an unnamed and secretive caste above the Elite, but there were those few who pulled the strings of the puppets in the government.

Few things survive catastrophes, among them, are cockroaches and the ultra-rich.

Unfortunately, the Envoy's pilot did not find his lot cast among the survivors once the fires in the terminal were extinguished. Shuttle destroyed and the charred remains of the pilot removed, Eli tutted and observed a forced moment of silence for the dead.

"I suppose I'll have to send word back for a replacement shuttle and pilot."

Not to be placed off his scheme, Pincer motioned a readied pair of security detail forward. Though they wore the colors of Protectorate officers, I did not recognize their rank insignia. The sign was that of the Greek letter Omega, a language I studied as a youth. I had no time to think about the significance.

"These guards will see to your safe return home using a craft of my own shuttle fleet." Pincer turned his plotting gaze to me. "First Protectorate MacKenzie Dillon here will escort you."

What was he up to, I wondered as my eye caught several cargo canisters being moved off the platform. McCord must have planned this with Pincer. I remembered then that McCord said he made arrangements for me to fly the Envoy somewhere. I was surprised by the methods and the disregard for life.

McCord notified me that this wasn't part of the plan. The sabotage was supposed to only disable the shuttle, but Pincer took the idea too far.

The containers being moved were not of Republic manufacture, which led me to turn my gaze toward the Envoy. Remembering that he mentioned there was more than the dusty old Hollywood star that he brought with him, I began to see the duality of his visit. The only thing the New Republic traded in those days was technology and medical advancements. Advancements from which only the Elite would benefit.

The New Republic had little need for tech originating from other Earth countries unless it was something built from reverse engineered plunder of the Space Force encounters out among the stars. An itching worry haunted the wonders of what could possibly warrant the need to trade with the Old Union. Until this day, the New Republic vehemently denied the existence of survivors from the Unifying Event as fake news. The catastrophe that was orchestrated through a tantrum by President of the United States of America. He blew up half the country to deny them the chance to secede. What unthinkable madness would bring the Lord Chancellor to re-embrace those who he played off as extinct? And why would a people who survived such treachery be inclined to barter?

I failed to notice the stillness of my surroundings. The Envoy and Vice Chancellor both gazed at me with quiet contemplation. I knew they both were vying for my loyalty. I felt then that my choices were easy. I would go with the Resistance and see where the Envoy might be ready to assist. Though my instincts were biting at my innards, warning me to deal with the devil I know.

The Vice Chancellor looked from me to the cargo and back at the Envoy.

"At least the…packages you brought us were removed safely before this unfortunate…malfunction," The Vice Chancellor said.

"Yes, rather fortuitous indeed," answered the Envoy.

"Unfortunate, however, is that the mechanism for unlocking the containers was in possession of my pilot, who was not as lucky to escape unharmed."

A moment of hesitation revealed the planning of the VC was not ready for such a move by Eli. I watched the two men locked in a mental game of chess. The Envoy, Eli Minsk just put the Vice Chancellor in check.

I followed as we walked nearer the containers hovering on an anti-gravity sled. They were now on the other side of the platform, away from the smoldering heap of melted alloys that was the Envoy's shuttle. The panel near the doors of each container displayed lights. There was also a slot for some sort of key-card.

"No matter," said Pincer. "We can simply use a plasma torch or other such device to cut them open."

Tutting escaped the Envoy's lips. "I would advise against that. You see we have lost items in the past in transit—hijackings in the wastes—so we have created these new vessels to be tamper proof. Try to force them open and…well, I would not want to be within a few hundred yards of the results. IT would be much larger than what happened to my ship."

Check Mate, I thought. And by the souring expression on Pincer's face, I saw how apropos his name suited.

"Commander, a word—please." The VC added the please with a tongue swollen from biting.

As I followed Pincer down the corridors, I noticed the thinning of his hair and the concave depth of his neck. The 'Elevens' on the back of one's neck usually came with age and frailty. Granted the Vice Chancellor was old at over 220 years, but with the longevity treatments and medical technology at his disposal, could it be some sickness?

Pincer turned and cleared his throat. The daggers from his stare told me he sensed I saw the state of his appearance. The VC forced a smile and leaned close to me.

"You will see to the Envoy's needs during the flight home. I have sent for one of my luxury shuttles. It is lavish if not slow so there will be plenty of time to pander to his left-coast ways and frivolous need for driveling niceties."

The Vice Chancellor waited a moment before widening his ice-blue eyes expecting my acknowledgment.

"Yes, Vice Chancellor."

"Good. While you are en-route, I want you to find the control key for these containers. I do not believe for a moment that such a thing would have been left with his servant."

"You think he's lying then?" I asked…stupidly it seemed.

I received a shockingly weak smack to the side of my head.

"Of course he's lying. All his kind lie and deceive. The complete downfall of the greatest nation on the planet and the known galaxy was due to his kind and their liberalism. The fact that we need… just perform as you are duty-bound and retrieve the card."

"If I am to pilot-"

"One of my men escorting you will pilot. The other will be there to take care…see to the Envoy and your return."

The Vice Chancellor ushered me back to the Envoy who waited surprisingly calm and smiling. He turned to us, pointing toward the arriving shuttle.

"I imagine this is the vessel you have chosen for us to return me home, Vice Chancellor."

"Indeed, Mr. Minsk. Only the best for our friends in the Old Union."

"Friends—Why does that word sound so dirty escaping your lips, Damien," Eli said. He spoke to the VC with a familiarity to his voice, old rivals or one final jibe at Pincer.

Pincer pursed his lips and waived his men over to take the shuttle controls and ushered us into the craft.

"Good travels," Pincer said and turned without waiting for a response.

I entered the shuttle and sat behind the controls in a pilot seat. I pulled Tinker's device from my jacket and began to place it beneath the console and fumbled. As the doors closed, one of the guards grasped my shoulder. I managed to get a firm connection for the device and made like I was preparing the lift-off protocols.

"Please sit back there. We leave at once."

***

The departure from the space station was less bumpy than I once remembered. Supposing that the difference in the method of transport had much to do with my comfort, I looked around the lavishly appointed vehicle.

Though there were clean lines, and the standards set up to any transport, the look of the technology was utterly foreign. Being used to personal shuttles and troop transports of the Protectorate, I actually thought it was just my lack of exposure to luxury vehicles. My attempts to get a look at the controls received two dirty looks from the Vice Chancellor's goons. What I could see was the touch panels, and maneuvering controls spoke of advancements that I was unaware.

More than once I glanced at the Envoy to see that he was watching me with interest. He seemed to be amused at my confusion with the technology. When he asked me if I was in need of refreshment, I thought it a simple empty question. That was until I saw him approach a panel opposite the reclined leather seat he removed his entitle ass from.

The leather was not worn or cracked as most reclaimed and reused materials have been. Sources of natural leather were non-existent in the New Republic, so either we were trading with other countries in secret, or there was some way to reverse time on old cow-hide pulled from the seats of an antique sedan. There were plenty old cars at the junk reclamation plants in the wastes.

The Envoy knew his way around the controls and amenities as he slid back a door on the side below a viewport. Within were a control pad and about a foot and a half cubed space. He punched a few buttons, and the area within lit up and beams of light dimmed to reveal a fabricated bottle of some liquor. Bourbon, I was told, is easily created from sacks of raw materials that such a replication device needs to build whatever you request.

"Nothing terribly original," the Envoy said. "This technology was dreamed about based on old television shows. There really are few original thinkers in the world these days. We do our best at the recycling of old ideas and materials then pass them off as new and innovative to mindless fools that you call the general public or grunts."

"You seem to know your way around this allegedly New Republic vehicle," I said. "How is that I've never seen these things and you seem completely at home?"

"OK, so it's Q and A time." Eli said as he poured us both a glass. "How about we do a bit of quid pro quo? I answer yours, and you answer mine."

"Ask what you like. I am a Protectorate soldier and servant of the New Republic," I said.

I kept my tone even and glanced at the Vice Chancellors men and back at the Envoy.

After looking at the men, the Envoy smiled at me and slid something over across our shared table.

"This would be what they are here for," Eli spoke low as not to be overheard. "You do know they will kill us both for that?"

"I'm not as dull as I might appear," I answered before taking a large gulp of the whiskey.

"Oh, you do not look dull to me at all young man. On the contrary. Everything Nathaniel has said so far seems undersold. Perhaps you'll grant me liberties to experience the rest."

"Oh for fuck's sake, is everyone wrapped up in the Resistance sexually-"

"Ambiguous...free thinking...open to new and sensual experiences? Pretty much, yes."

I wasn't sure how to respond to such a forward answer, so I decided to ignore it. "I imagine you have a plan then? Because I-"

The transport took a hard turn as we banked toward the middle of the wastes while entering the Earth's atmosphere. When I recovered from my fall to the floor, I felt the pull on my neck before I realized I was being choked.

I glanced at the Envoy who was sitting without care on his ass while the other VC guard reached toward him. I only remember the sickly sweet smell from a light mist filling the chamber as the lights faded from my eyes.

Chapter 16

"Wake up handsome, I need a bit of help here."

I cleared the crud from my eyes and gagged after coughing on the cold air surrounding us.

"Sorry about the theatrics," said the envoy. "It seems as though the Vice Chancellor has lost his touch."

"What's going on," I said.

"Well, we're about to crash if you don't get your fine ass off the ground young man."

While, I took the controls of the shuttle I looked at Eli and watched as he sat back and started picking at his nails as though nothing were going on at all. Now that I had a proper look at the controls I saw exactly how completely foreign they were to my training. However, they seemed similar in placement, so it wasn't long before I was able to gain control and level out our descent.

"Don't get too comfortable Dillon," the Envoy said. "I'm sure there were life sign transponders in these poor unfortunate lackeys."

"What the fuck does that mean."

"It means that the ship will probably self-destruct the engines because these dullards are dead."

I wasn't able to respond to Eli's statement as a moment later the ship's engines failed. We were plummeting toward the vast deluge of volcanic ash, snow and decay that filled most of the Midwest of the old United States now known as the Wastes.

Not waiting for me to ask what to do, the Envoy grabbed my wrist and pulled me toward the back of the vehicle. He shoved me into a small room that contained a couple seats. After pushing me into one and then sitting himself in the other, the seatbelts automatically wrapped around us and the little pod ejected.

Escape pods were not standard equipment on any New Republic transports. The question in my mind must've resonated to my face because the envoy answered it without me even asking.

"Who do you think built this thing," Eli asked. "There's a reason why I was so familiar with it, it's modeled after my own."

"Well thanks for that quid pro quo," I started. "And to answer yours, no you can't see my junk."

"We are plummeting toward a probable death, and you think I still want to see your cock. I can see why Nathaniel likes you."

I started laughing. "But you do don't you."

The ride got too bumpy and loud to hear or expect a response. Although I had trained for possible crash landings in my years before serving the Protectorate, we were never trained to use escape pods since they were not part of our equipment. Though now I know that escape pods are part of any transport that carries the Elite. Let everyone else die as long as the rich survive.

Far too many things crossed my mind as we were darting

towards the earth at thousands of miles an hour. The bone-jarring jerk of emergency parachutes slowed our descent. It doesn't matter how many parachutes you have, landing hard on the ground strapped inside an oversized tin can will knock the sense out of anyone.

I don't know how much time passed before I regained consciousness, but when I awoke to find ourselves firmly back to Earth, I didn't like what I saw.

The Envoy was bleeding badly. Though I only just met the man I knew he was the best chance and probably part of the financial backing to the Resistance. He may not have been the man in charge of the Old Union, but he was indeed high up in the echelon. I couldn't let him die not to mention I didn't want to think about being alone out in the middle of the Wastes.

As I pulled the Envoy free of his restraints and lay him flat on the pod floor to nurse his wounds, the fiery light of our once luxurious transport shown through the single window of our ride to uncertainty. We were alive, and the Envoy would survive, but we were in the middle of fucking nowhere surrounded by decaying buildings, dusty bones, and the remains of what the mad Lord Dampnut destroyed.

We no longer measure time with the term generations since those with means are able to manipulate how long they live. And as people live longer, at least those who can afford it, even the term decades has less meaning. So the measurement of time has altered the longer you're able to count the faces that come and go from existence. When I say that to look upon the decaying society that once existed around where we landed and think that how many generations had passed since this was a flourishing society seems...I can't express the hollowness I felt.

I walked out of the pod leaving Eli to heal and rest. I looked at our surroundings to see what must have once been a flourishing town or thriving metropolis. All that remained was nothing more than heaps of rusting or dusty old metal flakes and husks of what was once considered the height of civilization.

What we once thought—or at least those before me thought—as the top of the food chain in that prior civilization was now just dust and bones covered in ash and snow. All of this created by the greed and lust for power and control of those who feel that they are more capable of deciding how life and liberty should be dealt.

Hypocrisy, it leaves a trail of dust and destruction by those who blaze a path overtop anyone standing in their way to self-delusion.

As I looked around and felt the stirring in my bowels, I recognized the disgust I felt now knowing that this was all caused by design. I hadn't noticed the Envoy walking up behind me.

"It's hard to think that one man caused all this?" Eli asked.

"One man can do a great many evils, but I think it takes a lot more than what that limp-dick orange fool of a leader was capable when this all happened."

The Envoy looked me in the eyes and waited a moment, examining me. "You are far more intelligent than I suspected."

"I've heard whispers of an upper caste, those who really control things."

"Dillon, there's one thing that you need to understand. Asking questions outside of what your duty entails, can bring about your untimely demise. Take this place we landed, do you even know what this place was?"

"Some small city, a place where people lived and died, not knowing how little they meant to the men who orchestrated their demise."

"Oh, these people knew in the end who betrayed them. This was a place that good people came to die."

I looked at the Envoy, Eli, waiting for a further explanation but it did not come. He just looked away and went back to the pod and grabbed a tablet.

"What the hell is going on?"

The Envoy didn't answer. He just looked at his tablet, punched a few buttons and scowled. Eli threw the tablet down and actually started to express worry on his face.

"Are you seriously going to ignore my question?"

"We have bigger problems right now Dillon. At least one of the two escorts we had and thought I'd dispatched isn't exactly what he appeared. We're going to have company soon."

Before I could ask anything, we found ourselves under fire. Weapons usually reserved for border disputes or those that were allowed to be carried by the members of the New Republic were for stunning. Deadly weapons were just simple ballistic, old-fashioned bullet and gunpowder relics. We were being assaulted by energy weapons.

"What the hell are they shooting at us?" I asked.

"Prototypes of some of the things that I brought with me to the New Republic in those crates. Weaponry and technology reengineered from the spoils of Space Force conquests among other things."

We dove down behind the wreckage of what was once an old Volkswagen Beetle, ancient even in the times that I was a child. As we moved from place to place, cover to cover, the shots still rang out and followed our retreat to the pod.

Once we were back inside the pod and the door closed, the firing ceased.

"Why is he stopped firing?" I asked.

"Oh I'm sure he hasn't, but the dampening fields on this pod will prevent the firing from affecting the structure of our refuge."

I thought for a moment maybe more before I spoke out. "Exactly how long has the Old Union been trading with the New Republic?"

"We never stopped."

Eli's response was so matter-of-fact that I felt like I was an idiot for not understanding what was going on.

All at once it dawned on me that the New Republic, the Old Union—all of it—was tied to those who are still in control. The Oligarchy that started this, the self-involved, self-centered, self-elevating and self-deluding bastards, they still had power, and they were still trying to reshape everything to suit their own agendas.

"You were once one of the richest people in the world, are you part of this?"

"Better to work with the devils you know and try to change things from within than to outwardly disagree and be eliminated before you even get to start playing the game."

"So you were part of this, all of this from the beginning?"

The Envoy looked at me, and I could see pity in his eyes which made me that much angrier.

"Don't look at me like I'm a fucking idiot. Just tell me what your part in this was before I decide whether or not to kill you now."

"You could kill me I suppose because I stood by and let things happen. But had I spoke up then I'd be dead long before now and not here to help you make a change."

"And exactly what changes do you expect me to be able to bring?"

"Whatever change you like. Bring in a new guard? Eliminate the fool that runs your country? Hunt down the Oligarchy?"

"But according to you he was never in charge so why would I bring down the Lord Dampnut? He's never been the problem only the face of it."

"Again Nathaniel's assessment is correct, you are brilliant and obviously learning from what you have read on the device we made sure you got."

Eli's statement reminded me of the device I still carried within my coat. I pulled the communication device scavenged from the old shop and repaired by Tinker. Not entirely shocked that it was still functional this far outside of the Republic and away from the borders of the Old Union, I engaged the interface.

I was surprised at the time by the change in the display and those options available, but understanding now that this was all by design it made no difference at that moment. Without thinking, I pressed the red button that appeared and labeled distress.

"What have you pressed on the device there Dillon," asked Eli.

"I think I've called for help."

"Without understanding who might answer?" Eli asked. "There's only so much I can preplan for, such as pre-rigging this pod for our survival, making sure there was an escape plan programmed into our transport, but also having my own backup rescue."

Chapter 17

Though the pod we were encased in blocked out much of the noise, the firefight that began outside was not muffled beyond our hearing. As I inched up to the one viewport in the pod to examine what was going on outside all I could see was energy from weapons fire being sent between multiple vantage points.

Not only was our pursuer from the original transport crash still out there where we left him, but there were also at least two new sides entered into the fray. Unsure what to do we remained within the pod until the side of our shelter blew open from a blast.

Our transport was no longer adequate shelter from the firefight. I looked out the hole and saw a small outbuilding with a steel door hanging open. I mentioned the run for cover to Minsk, but I didn't wait for Eli to answer and ran.

Dodging fire from one end of the fighting, both Eli and I

managed to make it into the small structure and pulled the door closed. The first thing I noticed was the ash and bones we were standing in.

"What the hell?" I said.

Eli gasped when he picked up some ash and moved it around in his hand. Teeth remained in Eli's palm after the ash fell away.

"This is one of Dampnut's death camps. We're inside a crematory furnace."

I didn't know whether to run or vomit first. The firing of weapons outside kept us inside the furnace against my desire to get away from the horror within. I choked down my bile and decided to try and block the images out of my mind, but it was futile. I looked around the interior of our alleged safety to taste irony in the stirred up ash on my lips.

Eli let out a sardonic laugh. "A homo and a foreigner walk into an oven…"

I knew his poor attempt at tasteless humor was to lighten the mood, but it was too surreal. I could see images playing in my mind of the last moments these unfortunate souls endured. Burned alive for nothing more than speaking up, loving the wrong person, wanting freedoms and equality…the results of rebuilding a nation using hate.

We sat in silence for the dead while waiting for silence from outside.

Banging on the furnace door finally pulled me from my internalizing the events of the day. I had no way of knowing who was on the opposite side of the door because there was no window or way to communicate externally. I opened the door on the hope that it was someone who could help.

One can only imagine the shock that I felt when I looked down to find a familiar face and one that I wouldn't expect so far out into the middle of the Wastes. Lucas smiled up at me.

"What you sitting in here for Dillon? All the fun is outside," Lucas said.

"Lucas, what are you doing here?" He was with Samuel and others I did not know.

"Tinker added that extra little button for distress so that in case you needed us we'd know where to find you."

Though I was relieved to find out that my pushing of the button brought about friendly assistance, it did little to soothe my worry over this young boy being in the middle of my fight to live. We were overlapping an otherwise preplanned escapade of the Envoy and whatever game he was playing with Pincer.

"So who are the other people out there firing?" I asked.

Samuel glanced from me to the Envoy. "That would be his people."

Lucas glared at the Envoy. "Would you mind calling them off?"

Eli grunted and then pushed a button on the device he revealed from beneath his lapel. Outside, the firing ceased.

Before long both parties met outside the death chamber. Though tensions were soothed by the Envoy and my presence, an animosity ingrained in the differences between the New Republic and anyone outside it remained, particularly Elite outsiders.

The Envoy's men all began to gather and then called in for their transport to take the Old Union forces and their leader home. The Envoy and his company started to walk away before Eli turned back and gestured for me to join him a moment.

Eli handed me the control card for the crates that were delivered by his destroyed shuttle.

"Take this, it will open the remaining crates. I'm going to leave it up to you to decide what to do with the card's auxiliary contents."

"Why give this to me? You brought that shipment to the Vice

Chancellor. You meant for him to have whatever is inside."

"If you haven't discovered by now, not everything is always what it seems."

The Envoy looked at me and then pointed down to what remained of the soldier that accompanied us on our original departure from the space station. The skin was melting away to reveal a mechanized interior.

"He's an android?" I asked.

"Yes, sentinel model. Some of what's in those crates is something far more advanced and far more difficult to dispatch."

"And why would you give such a thing to the New Republic?"

Eli looked at me and laughed. "You forget I told you, better the devil you dance with under the light of knowledge than to gyrate alone in the darkness of ignorance. One never knows how to prepare for the future if they don't know what's coming."

Before I could question further, Eli turned and left with his company in their shuttle. I was left alone wondering what the hell he actually meant surrounded by unfamiliar faces, filthy faces of those who obviously lived out in the Wastes rather than behind the fantastic walls of protection called the New Republic.

"Where the hell are we, Lucas? Samuel?"

"Outside of what used to be called Denver," Samuel said. "Come on, we'll take you to a stronghold of the Resistance in this area."

I followed Samuel, Lucas and their friends to a nearby ground vehicle. It appeared a jumbled mess of repurposed parts and welded-on accessories, but inside it was not that uncomfortable. It wasn't pristine and new such as the craft I abandoned mid-trip in favor of surviving in a pod. That is after crashing to the ground. This transport was a heap, but it wasn't lined with benches and straps as I had imagined.

Old bucket seats from cars were bolted unevenly across both sides of the interior. View screens lined the opposite sides of each row so we could view the broadcasts from the Republic as we traveled to the rebel stronghold.

As we began our departure, Samuel and Lucas told me some of the history about their acquaintances and the people who still lived out in the Wastes.

Lucas was excited to tell me all about the people that he worked with, all throughout the alleged wastelands. They were a strong and stalwart group. All descendants from the original families who survived the fallout from the Unifying Event; they kept detailed records of all that occurred since the eruption of Yellowstone. These survivors knew the partial truth of what happened. Now with the added knowledge of Dampnut having pushed the button, they were more determined than ever.

"We have been preparing to retake the country for decades," Samuel said. "All our family lines have been collecting weapons and supplies for generations. Our time is nearing."

I got a rundown of the inventory they had stockpiled. Everything the Resistance needed to storm the Wall and begin retaking the New Republic was accounted for. The biggest problem they would face was the Wall itself. It was heavily guarded and fortified, but Samuel assured me there were more than a few insiders working the problem. When the time was right, their agents would act.

"Thanks to a steady supply of contraband we've acquired and the added support we have from an alliance with the UN," Samuel started.

"Wait," I said. "The UN is involved?"

"They are a silent supporter to our cause. Of course, the UN can not openly support us, but they have seen to it we have assistance. Once the Resistance retakes the New Republic, the UN is prepared to reopen talks and become more active in rebuilding."

Lucas kept asking when we attack and how we could blow up the wall. I had to admire his moxie, but he was just a kid. I looked around at the faces of my companions. They were all so very young, even those that were of middle-age compared to myself. Life was rough out in the Wastes, even with shelter and support. These people did not have longevity nor did they have the same medical attention as those in the New Republic. Children were forced to grow up quickly in this new world.

Noting my worried look for these kids, Lucas came over and sat by me.

"Don't you worry Mr. Mac. We are smart, and we can do what is asked of us."

"But most of you are all just children."

Lucas looked at me then backed away. "We are no less capable than you old farts."

I tried to take my foot out of my mouth, but Lucas still yelled at me for nearly thirty minutes. He spoke of how he and his fellow 'children' were able to go places and do things that adults could not. They were smaller and able to hide and go unseen more easily. They could fit between the secret pathways through the Great Wall and swim beneath water longer to sneak things in and out of the New Republic.

Children get ignored in the New Republic when covered in grime and looking every part the Grunt. They are only precious when they are babies and possible brats to be adopted by the barren Elite. Kids of Lucas's age are unwanted if they are not already conscripted into the Protectorate or other services. They just move about like any other slave to the nation.

Though I wish I had the time to listen to all of Lucas's tale, it was wasting. The broadcast being played now meant that there was no way I would make it all the way to the Denver stronghold.

"Stop the vehicle," I said.

"What's wrong Mr. Mac?" Lucas asked.

I pointed at the screen to instruct that he should listen.

The headline read First Prime missing along with a diplomat, followed by the Press Secretary announcing that rebels may be involved. It didn't look good for the party I was with or me. For that matter mentioning rebels didn't bode well for the Press Secretary.

Chapter 18

The Chancellor's broadcast made my job that much more difficult. Beside the fact he presented as more deranged than usual, his introduction of Drucilla Cordwin as his interim Press Secretary gave me pause.

In light of my situation, I found it humorous that even the rebels were taking bets on how long it would be before the newest Press Secretary was killed. Mentioning revolution or revolutionaries was as forbidden as talking about abortion.

"You need to let me out here. There's no time to take me back to the wreckage."

"Too risky," Samuel said. "We should continue on or leave you for dead here."

"Don't be wasteful and stupid," Lucas said. "We need Dillon."

I used my OU device to clone the security card that Eli gave me. While that was processing, I noticed files that transferred as well and then got deleted from the card. I had no time to examine the contents or make any other changes to my hasty plan. I handed the device to Lucas.

"Take this and get it back to me later. I can't be found with it."

Lucas took the device and winked before reaching over to me while the transport doors opened. He tore parts of my uniform. As I prepared to jump out, I looked at Samuel as he approached, knowing his mind.

"Make it look convincing," I said.

As I saw the man's arm swing around, the gleam of the metal instrument in Samuel's hand was the last I recalled before waking up in a pile of snow.

Hearing the approach of a shuttle, I immediately realize that Lucas must have reactivated my pendant. I had deactivated it shortly before leaving with the Envoy thinking best we not be tracked. Now I actually wanted to be found before I died of starvation or froze to death. The thawing in the wastes was slow over the last century. But at the elevation near Denver, I was in the middle of a blizzard.

I looked around to gauge direction or anything to identify where I was, but the elements battled my senses.

The wind that whipped up and spun around me caused noises to echo from all directions. I used my scarf to help cover my face but still choked on the frigid air I took in. I had no way to identify what direction the shuttle was approaching from and no sense of where they might land.

The Wastes; there was more devastation out here than the exploding supervolcano explained. This type of unchallenged flow of air meant there were no structures, no landmarks, nothing except flat empty snow-covered land.

I could tell a shuttle landed nearby, there was no mistaking the sound of the extending landing gear. I heard shouting and footsteps just before a firm grasp lifted me to my shaky feet. I was escorted, more to the point dragged, to my would-be rescue craft only to find the Vice Chancellor sitting before me. I delayed his inquiry as I cleared the melting snow and ash from my eyes.

"Did you get it?" Pincer asked.

Not that I expected him to ask how I was doing, but if you can act the part of second in charge to those who serve the Protectorate, I would've hoped he'd at least fake concern.

I handed the card over to the Vice Chancellor.

"Not without some great difficulty, least of which came from your escort who interfered and ultimately caused our crash."

I knew I was setting the fire on my own tightrope, but I felt a bit of indignation was warranted. I don't know what I expected from Pincer as a response, but he remained cold and focused on what he wanted. Pincer waved off the actions of his men as inexperience and confused by the orders they were given. I stopped myself before asking what orders those were.

"And what of the Envoy," Pincer asked.

Speaking faster than I could think, "Was he not there when you picked me up?"

Pincer narrowed his eyes at me and leaned forward. "You were found a fair distance from what remains of my best shuttle. He was not with said shuttle, nor where we finally picked up your location."

I shrugged. "I remember taking the card from Eli, then coming under attack from one of your men, then...I have bits of flashes walking."

"Are you claiming amnesia?" Pincer snapped.

I paused only a moment before wording things correctly. "I'm saying it has been a long night and that I don't recall clearly at the moment. Perhaps this bleeding lump on my head has something to say?"

Pincer sent back and looked at me, pushing a false look of concern on his face. He motioned an onboard medic to come take a look at me and clean up my wounds.

The male nurse looked familiar to my clouding eyes, but I could not focus as the syringe entered my skin. As my surroundings faded, I glanced over at Pincer who continue to look at me without hiding his skepticism. As if my body responded to my wish of feigning weakness, I passed out from whatever was pumped into my veins.

***

I awoke in a stark white, sparse and sterile room with a Protectorate guard snoozing in the corner. A young recruit I saw a few times, but not on familiar terms. When he noticed I was stirring, he called into his com device that I was awake.

As I propped myself up, I was greeted by the warm and cheerful face of McCord. By warm I mean unreadable and by cheerful I mean pissy.

"You look no worse for wear."

"I feel…actually I feel fine, except for a slight ring in my ears." I reached to touch my head wound to find it completely healed. "How long have I been here?"

"Just a couple hours," McCord said. "The ringing will eventually subside."

Medical advancements aside, I would have expected to feel some aches or even tenderness where my head should have hurt. I felt like a new man.

McCord made little waste of time in pulling my uniform out, fully repaired and cleaned, and told me to get dressed.

"Time for you to get back to work," McCord said. "We have detainees suspected to be Resistance members or sympathizers in custody."

"Shit," I said aloud. "Um, I mean, that was fast."

McCord laughed as he dismissed the rookie guard. "They were already detained on other charges. The Vice Chancellor wanted swift action, and we have to give him results fast."

"So these people are not-"

"These people are criminals for certain and will face death regardless. We will provide them a means to a fast and merciful end."

The change in McCord's tone was surprising, but I was pained more by my agreement. Whatever menial offense they made, that in old-law would have meant probation or a few years incarceration, now meant slave labor or death. Prisons were no longer a profit industry when faced with reduced resources and the need for procreating capable people. Money was not made on isolating and punishing the masses. Money or credits as it was now traded, was in making more babies to grow up and serve the New Republic.

Crimes committed meant you were either sent to the Wastes to salvage, sent to reconditioning to become a soldier in the Protectorate, or used as repro-meat. Reproduction facilities harvested sperm and eggs from criminals to produce viable fertilized embryos to the Elite who could not reproduce because of the effects of anti-aging. You fuck with Mother Nature, and she'll fuck back harder.

McCord helped me dress and soon pulled me along to the medic desk and signed me out.

My release was quick and without fuss. I felt as though the

person signing me out was glad to see the bed open. When I looked at the chart, I saw the woman check a box reading reset, but was moved along before I could get a better look.

McCord rushed me back to headquarters where he placed me at my appointed seat as First Protectorate.

"Time to sit in judgment and do your duty," McCord said with a wink.

The man looked at me as though I should be preparing to enjoy myself. From the churning, in my gut, I felt prepared to lose my lunch, but I didn't remember the last time I ate.

My thoughts of lacking appetite evaporated as the guards brought in a line of detainees.

Ages ranged from late teen to one woman who was middle-aged but looked as though every hard year of life formed its own crack along her face. Seeing these people and knowing their hardships, I couldn't help but compare them to those living outside the Wall. Two very similar ways of getting through life.

Outside the wall, they stole and scavenged and lived off the silent contributions of others. Inside the wall, they still scavenged and stole and lived off what others provide. The problem being is that those under the alleged protection of the Protectorate had it worse. They were slaves to the government that kept them ignorant.

These sorry and wasted human lives were controlled and fed on lies and had no dreams of a better life. They had no idea what a better life might be. At least on the outside, those people had the truth and a living history of how things used to be and could be again one day.

I listened to the court crier list out the charges against those lined up in my courtroom. I wanted nothing more than to dismiss all charges, but I couldn't.

I also couldn't bring myself to make a unilateral proclamation. I re-read over the array of violations, most being listed as inciting treason against the New Republic through forbidden speech. Others were for gathering in numbers higher than three in private. And a final was for painting a graven image of the Lord Chancellor as a diaper wearing orange pig playing in a pile of shit. I nearly laughed at the visual imagery, but managed to maintain.

I was expected to be swift and pass judgment. I was not willing to sell my soul, though I could not underplay my part. As I sat there staring at the sullen and dirty faces of the accused, not accused but already convicted without trial of the old courts, I decided not to send them to death.

I recalled an earlier news report in the dilapidated Resistance transport playing about a work transport that had crashed, killing all the passengers. There was a shortage of hands available, and all work would be halted on the Wall repairs as well as the other jobs left unfilled by the loss of labor. Grateful workers might be convinced to help place 'extra materials' inside the Wall.

"I sentence you all to hard labor among the work corps. You will replenish the losses to the Wall work force."

The silence in the room made the ringing in my ears sound like an orchestra of wind chimes. There were a few murmurs among the crowd, those who expected a show of killing, but none would question the word of the First Protectorate Commander. Not in my presence at any rate.

The guards ushered the line of new workers out of my court. A few looked at me before bowing their heads. One middle-aged woman maintained eye contact, her expression reading as a wish to have been sent to her death.

I wondered whether it was a favor I granted these poor souls, or a sentence worse than death. They would be worked until they died all the same if things did not change soon.

This among many things kept me up that night.

Chapter 19

I walked the streets of the ground level that evening, the first of many. Since sleep wasn't coming easy that night and most nights, I thought I'd make good use of my fantastic energy. Whatever rejuvenation treatment I received at the healing center had long-lingering effects on my body and mind. It was rare that I felt no fatigue or any aches and pains. Even for a man of over one hundred fifty years on the longevity treatment, I should feel something of my age.

The more I thought about that, the more my ears started to ring. The one side effect of being healed that was not going away was that blasted high-pitched, incessant ringing. I needed this walk around the General Population to clear my head and focus on something else.

Taking a seat at a refreshment trailer, I ordered what passed for coffee in the lower levels and took out the device that Lucas managed returning to me earlier in the day. The files that transferred from Eli's security key displayed on the screen, taunting me to open and reveal their secrets. None of the data contained anything I could find about the cargo delivered in the crates. They were all video files perhaps meant to leave a clue. I had no idea what the Envoy hoped to share with me.

I opened the first file, to find another old-style newsreel video clip. The recording was of a reporter out in the field, a storm of roiling and electrically charged clouds filling the skies behind her. She spoke of the madness of the President and his actions to retain control. The Unifying Event as would later be rewritten to suit the New Republic agenda was all orchestrated by the President. I had to ask myself why. I did not want to believe what I was seeing and hearing again, but part of me chewed on the truth of this *real news*.

Having lost the majority of control in the house of government and the prospect of re-election unlikely, the President—in his madness—set to take what he wanted.

While the legislative bodies were all on a break and back home with their families, the President enacted his plan. Using the newly established Space Force, he gained access to a planetary monitoring system that was a cover for a weapons platform. The Rod from God system is what changed the face of the Earth and was the beginning of the end for democracy.

A ten-ton tungsten rod was dropped from one-thousand kilometers at eleven kilometers per second. Thought to be environment-friendly, nobody foresaw what would happen if one was sent into the center of a supervolcano. Actually, at least one or more people thought about it and made sure the imbecile sitting in the White House heard whispers. He could not have imagined this plan up himself.

Whether in part or completely aware of the possibilities, the puppet masters who controlled the President made sure he had both a means to eliminate most of the opposing body from the House and Senate, and have just cause to impose martial law. There would be no election now.

Martial law remains, but now in the form of the Protectorate. Government reformed, the President named himself Lord Chancellor, and the rest is history. History continually altered to hide the truth and labeled as *fake news*.

At that moment I had a flashback of time with my parents just before the devastation that destroyed the United States and altered the face of the planet. My father was going on one of his tangents about how the people of this country were like beaten dogs.

My Father said, "A dog will keep going back to its master for attention and expecting better treatment, no matter how much it gets beaten back down. One day that dog needs to bite back."

My mother's response was always the same. "Those beaten dogs are too weak to fight as a pack or too frightened to see the monster that keeps them alive and fed just enough to beat them down again."

I saw the truth in those words for the first time as I watched the grungy and downtrodden Grunts walk past me. Keeping to themselves, afraid to engage or reach out for the company of others, they were every bit beaten dogs.

There was one set of eyes in the sea of soot-covered faces that met mine. Cold, I shivered from the glare that lingered and was gone when another group of laborers passed. The discomfort that remained on the back of my neck caused me to move. I was being watched, followed in spite of my disguise. At times I thought I could hear the breathing of my pursuer.

Walking the streets, keeping my pace and watching for a

trailing presence, I barely registered the buzzing from my OU device. Ducking into a doorway of an abandoned side street, I opened the screen to see Nate smiling back at me.

"How did you-"

"No time love. You are being followed."

"No shit."

Nate smirked. "I should have guessed you'd figure that out. Come to the club. There was a woman here looking for you. She said she would be back in the early hours."

"Who?"

"Just come." Nate winked at me then disconnected.

The screen went black, and I tucked it away before checking my path. I made my way through the streets to the nearest express lift back to the upper levels of the city. Using these lifts was a risk in my current garb, so I quickly made a change and removed the appearance altering tech. As I approached the elevator, I turned, feeling a presence behind me. There was no-one, but I saw something shift in the shadows. I was stopped from investigating by the deep throat rumbling of a lift guard.

"First Protectorate, I didn't know you were out. Where is your personal escort?"

I scowled at the man. Though he wore the clothing of the Protectorate, his face was sullen and he was dressed as a drafted Grunt raised to a level above his birth. What secrets did he sell to the Protectorate for this reward?

"I need not share my movements with my subordinates, nor do I require a company to assist in my inquiries."

The guard stiffened and shut his mouth. He was new to the post and not yet broken in by his superiors. Questioning anyone above his station would be a hard lesson, but not one I had the stomach to teach. I chose words over fist.

"If you wish to remain in your current station, I will advise you learn not to speak to your betters unless instructed to do so. And never question the actions of your Commander. I serve the Nation above all."

I pushed past him as he gave me a wide berth. As I entered the lift, I turned for the retinal scan and saw those eyes again piercing through the dark. The red beam in my eye prevented me from seeing my stalker's face. As the lift doors closed, I saw him inching out of the shadows, but not clearly. The doors sealed, and I was being hurtled some ninety stories upward into the upper city. Identifying my stalker would have to wait.

***

I made it back to my chambers without further delay or sign of being followed. I knew I wasn't paranoid at least. I had every reason to have suspicion placed upon me. I was a highly placed officer of the Protectorate and not from a wealthy family. I was not above the same laws I pretended to believe were gospel. Only those born to the few families of means and power could get away with anything and not face persecution.

With time to kill before heading out to meet Nate and the mystery woman, I sat the OU device down and linked it to my display screen on the far wall. Using the holo-display controls, I swiped through the files revealing more images of horror in the aftermath of the Yellowstone explosion.

Digital footage played of the last century and a half of how the face of the continent was altered and civilization nearly wiped out. But out of the ash, life was rebuilding out in the Old Union. This was well hidden from the New Republic citizenry. I had no doubt that the leaders and those in control knew all about the rebuilding going on in the west.

Something I had not expected to witness was people of all background, color, creed, religion, orientation…none of that mattered when working toward survival. The contents of these recordings showed how the Old Union worked together to survive and thrive.

There was abundant food being farmed and ample water being reclaimed from deep wells and filtration plants that now peppered the western planes and mountains. The technology companies that survived in California consolidated into a single organization focused on adapting to the needs of the people and creating machines to clean up the mess made by the mad President.

I watched a documentary on the company, lead by Eli Minsk, charging ahead with developing technologies to better the human existence. The man looked the same then as he did when last I saw him. The technology and medical treatments for longevity were not a New Republic secret. The questions began to race through my mind. This film was from at least seventy years past. If the man was ageless then, how long ago was there trading of information going on?

Then I saw a symbol on the side of an early model shuttlecraft. The same logo was on the OU device now in my possession and on the crates delivered by the Envoy. I know I had seen that symbol at other times as well but could not place it until I went to put on my jacket.

As I prepared to leave for my meeting with Nathaniel, I saw the symbol in the lapel pin I wore. Wrapped around the sword was the symbol for Omega. That was the same symbol on the Old Union cargo, the device, and those vehicles from the OU video archive files. There was trading going on with the West this entire time.

It was also the symbol of Vice Pincer's guards.

My anger began to bubble over as I wrapped my cloak around my shoulders. I grabbed the pin and disabled the tracking device, but held it a moment longer. Tech built by the Old Union and being used by the New Republic. What else was coming from them and what were we trading back to them? And how was it all linked? It had to be the rumored Omega Caste.

By the time I reached the club, I was reeling with conspiracy and collusion. I was careful in my travel, however, making sure to not have my shadow. I could little afford being linked to the club and its debaucherous tenants. The Elite could get away with what they liked, but at the end of the day, I was not one of them. My position was of little protection against the Edicts that would condemn the lessors of this New Republic.

Nate paused when he found me and looked into my eyes.

"What has you so ill-minded, my love?"

"Too much truth for one day," I answered a bit more terse than I would have preferred. "Sorry, I don't mean to take a poor tone with you, I just have found out some things I'm still digesting."

Nate pushed me into a chair before sitting in my lap.

I looked around to find the patrons too self-absorbed in their own pleasures to notice my discomfort in the public display. A display that would get anyone else immediately eradicated. Our supposed sickness would never be accepted in this society again. A problem that did not exist in the Old Union I imagined from what I viewed earlier in the evening.

Nate pressured me to share what burdened my mind, so I spoke about what was revealed in the videos. As I told him of the thriving society out west and how they have been there all along, I saw no surprise in Nate's face.

"You know about all this?" I said more than asked. "How long?"

"Dillon—Mac—this is nothing new. The acts of the man who

was President then and Lord Chancellor now were not done in a vacuum. Nor has any activities gone unknown or allowed since the Unifying Event."

"What does that mean?"

"What I am saying is that Dampnut was too stupid to pull off what happened, and the Old Union could not have survived if they were not prepared for what would come."

I blinked away the fog from my mind. "Collusion?"

"I don't know for certain, but I've spent a lot of time wondering about who really has the power of our puppet ruler and the clout to maintain trade this whole time with what remained of the United States. It has to be the Omega I've heard whispers of."

I shushed Nathaniel for saying too much that would get him killed, even as an Elite. The rumored Omega Caste, had to be at the center after hearing Nate's similar information.

"Never mind that now," Nate said and pulled me from my seat. "You have a visitor in the back room."

When we found ourselves tucked away from the crowd and noise of the main bar, I saw a shadow sitting in the dark corner of the back room. She moved out as Nate closed the door.

I recognized the eyes. Not those of my stalker, but the pleading eyes of the woman I so recently saved from death but condemned to a lifetime of labor. Though I did alter her assignment, she would serve the rest of her life in the service of the Protectorate as an indentured slave.

"How are you here?" I asked, "And why do you seek me out?"

She hesitated until Nate nodded that she could trust me.

"I know you saved my life and made sure I was assigned a less harsh service."

"It was the best I could achieve at the time."

She nodded her thanks and understanding. She reached into

her coat and pulled out a tablet.

"I stole this from crates because it looked important. When I brought it to our group, they told me to find the new Resistance leader. Nate said that was you."

I was a bit shocked, to say the least. The leader of the Resistance and First Commander to the Protectorate, how many faces must one wear to make a positive and drastic change?

"I am not sure I am the one you want to see," I said but then looked at the tablet.

An incomplete list and photos of a delivery. Some of the items from within the crates Eli delivered. The manifest along with a means of programming the devices and controlling their distribution. The container was also full of specialized missiles for delivering biotech weapons.

Chapter 20

What was Eli doing by presenting weapons to the New Republic and who was the target? The tablet the woman turned over had no details on what the purpose of the weapons ultimately was. When I looked up to question her, she was gone.

"Where did she go?"

Nathaniel shrugged and went to look for her. By the time he returned I was three drinks toward boozing my way into denial.

"You aren't going to solve your troubles in the swill they server at this place sweetness," Nate said. "Let's get out of here, and I'll give you a real drink."

I agreed. "I don't think there's any liquor in this bottle anyway. I don't feel a thing from it."

"What else are you feeling?" Nate asked as we walked to my shuttle. "I mean after your incident in the Wastes."

I told Nate about how I was feeling, particularly with the excess energy and inability to sleep. When I mentioned the constant ringing in my ears, he seemed a bit concerned for a moment before getting handsy.

"Well, I know a brilliant way to work off some of that excess energy."

I had to agree and was ready to strip him naked on the spot. I managed to maintain my lustful appetite long enough to reach my vehicle, but only just. As we set the craft to automatic pilot, we enjoyed the slow route back to the heights of a Florida city from the grunge of Old Manhattan. We were going to one of Nathaniel's other homes.

This far away from the North and West, the sky was more clear, and the rising sun set a spectacular show on the horizon. Blue ocean and cleaner air were reserved for only those with the means. What remained of the Florida coast after the pile of ash and changed weather, was coveted land. This corner of the country was reclaimed, cleaned and nearly good as new.

Built atop the old coastlines was the few and private mansions in the sky of the ultra-rich. Somehow, the art-deco world of former Miami rose above the ash and flooding to become a higher and more lavish place.

Ships that sailed as comfortably on both sea and air lined the new coast. All the luxuries that wealth could afford the wealthiest were found in this beautiful playground of the Elite. If the Grunts ever saw how their world could look, the revolution would be well underway.

I spared little more attention to my surroundings as we were approaching Nate's place. I was far too distracted by what he was doing to me. My blood was rushing throughout my stiffened body. Only the halt of our transport brought us out of mutual bliss.

We continued our engagement in lustful sin against society while discarding the rest of our clothing throughout the main floor of Nate's apartments.

My energy lasted throughout the entire day. Nate did his best to keep up.

As I sat watching the sun's last light fade, I wondered at how the colors played against the clear skies. I wondered at how my time in the Wastes was so different. So much of the continent remained unusable in spite of the efforts of the Old Union, but not all of it.

Nate slid in beside me on the comfortable and supple skinned sofa looking out on the coastal waters.

"What are you thinking?" Nate asked.

"Just wondering at how the Wastes still exist while this beauty has returned."

"Only parts of the Wastes remain if you believe what the old stiffs in charge ramble on about."

I looked at Nate and pressed for a further explanation. His father is among the Elite in council to the Lord Chancellor, meaning Nate was privy to more information than most.

"Father is always complaining about what to do about the clearing and reuse of land beyond our walls. It's getting more difficult to control information considering the number of Grunts that work the farms and mine for diamonds and silicon along the old scavenging routes."

"What farms?"

Nate told me about the lands cleared and used to begin new farming and cultivation outside the walls. While we had growing centers within our borders, the soil outside the Great Wall was far more fertile than before the eruption.

"Why hasn't this news been shared? Someone would have talked by now."

"The labor used on those farms lives on them. They couldn't be allowed to spread news of what is happening outside their trapped existence in the New Republic."

Nate raised his hands as I expressed horror for his words.

"Just quoting my father. I don't accept what is happening here. I think the wall should come down and people begin repopulating the useful land. But then whose backs would our society stand upon?"

"You mean who would the rich get to make their beds and serve them the good food coming from the farms?"

Nate rolled his eyes at me. "It's not a good or equal society, but it saw us through when the rest of the world turned their backs on us…or at least I'm told. Far before my time."

"Nate, you are young, and though you may have more information than most, it is still very one-sided."

"Look. I may be young and didn't live through what you did, but I know a few things too. For one thing, the kind of change you and the rest of the Resistance want does not come quickly or without heavy tolls."

"That does not mean we have time for tea and cakes while that spawn of the devil Vice Chancellor plans some other genocide with these new missiles from the Old Union." I tossed the tablet from that woman at Nate. "Have you seen what these things can do?"

Nate scanned over the information before handing me back the manifest. "What do you think? Can you stop him? You don't even know what they are for. Maybe we are under attack again from foreign nations."

Foreigners were not spoken of in the New Republic. They were not welcome to live within our borders and any visitors where only those with power or wealth that could be used. None ever stayed for long and said visits were never made public. The New Republic leadership knew how the rest of the world would continue to judge us if they saw how the citizens were forced to exist.

It was bad enough in the early days when the United Nations moved to South America and forced the United States out. All trade with the US ended except for Russia. Even China stopped communications and wrote off all debt. The United States was shunned by the world because of what one man did. We became the shit-hole country.

Karma is a vengeful bitch.

Nate and I argued the subtler points of what was wrong with the New Republic, which was nearly everything. When the subject of a better life came up, I told Nate of the videos I watched from the OU archives. He was interested but skeptical.

"Why do you suppose Eli made sure you got those files. Is he above manipulation of information? I know he isn't"

The truth was I didn't know what to think. I was placed in a position of power far above my station in life. I was being groomed as a Resistance leader by the very man who put me in charge of the Enforcers we'd be fighting. An ancient philanthropist with too much money has started plying me with information about the past. And then there was this handsome man leading me toward a chopping block with the forbidden love we felt for one another.

The ringing came back full-force. As I wiggled my finger in my ear, Nate leaned in.

"The ringing?"

"Yes, I don't understand why it persists."

Nate gave me a rub and handed me a drink.

"Drink this, it'll take the ringing away."

I drank the bourbon but tasted something more. Before I could say anything, my vision faded and the world went black and still.

***

When I woke later that day, it was in my own chambers. I had no memory of traveling home nor what day it was. After I checked the date and time, I was relieved to find it still my day off but surprised at my fatigue.

Everything hurt and I was the kind of tired I had not felt in a long time, oversleeping. Though I was not due at my appointed position as First Protectorate, I had work to accomplish in the lower levels.

I needed to find out what the missiles were for, organize the Resistance, and discover who was following me.

Lingering in the shower a bit longer than necessary, I felt the ease of my muscles under the hot water. I still felt discomfort in my limbs as I dried, but perhaps the days of not sleeping were catching up to me. When I wiped the mirror to look at my reflection, I was more perplexed by what stared back at me. I had sudden growth of facial hair, remembering I had not shaved in a couple days. Then there was the thin pink line above my right temple.

The place where I was hit by Samuel in the wastes, it left a small scar somehow even after my medical treatment. It was barely noticeable, but I couldn't understand how I missed finding it before now.

I had little time to spend with contemplating how a scar could have a delayed appearance or my beard magically growing overnight. My communication device had several messages from connections in the Resistance, so I had to apply my disguise and head out into the Grunt population.

Chapter 21

My disguises had to change along with where I went while patrolling the General Population. I never was sure what I hoped to find on those walks among the lower caste, but I certainly became more aware of their plight. I saw more clearly what deplorable living conditions passed as acceptable for all but the wealthy. I could not understand why the people didn't see the inequity themselves or instead chose to ignore it. The fact that there was no way of seeing how the upper castes lived was itself a means of control. You can't be envious of that which you can not witness. If the Grunts actually knew all the wonders and luxuries the Elite squandered and wasted, there would be no need to organize a resistance. The ninety-nine percent would overrun the entirety of the Elite and Protectorate before they knew what happened.

Though I walked new streets, I saw the same scene played by

different actors. The vacant looks and empty stares of the masses did little to ease my worry. But things began to change.

I began coming across individuals who needed help, and I offered it. Instead of stepping over a fallen Grunt, I helped them up. Rather than allow unjust treatment of the general citizenry at the hands of the Enforcers, I interceded. I did this both in disguise and as First Protectorate.

Those few numbers supporting the Resistance began growing as word spread of change coming. The people in the streets no longer feared when I made an appearance. I controlled my ranks. I managed their actions, I instilled new habits and ways of thinking. I was approachable and spoke words from the New Polari booklet McCord provided.

"Bona journo are you bencove?" Asking a vendor selling trinkets if he were a friend.

"Me bencove to nada the cra muppet."

He was a friend and not a fan of the mad leader. I nodded, bought one of his items, a little ring made of twisted wire. It was nothing fancy, but the ring had a charm that I admired. I put it on my pinky and moved along. Making my rounds, I stopped at many vendors and shops. I found who I could seek as a contact and whom to be wary. More often than not, I was regarded with skepticism and silence, but I noticed the look of hope starting to shine in the eyes of the people.

Eventually, more of the General Population started regarding my presence as welcome. I was given tidbits of information from the work of the Resistance and most importantly how well the children were doing.

Word spread of my involvement and leadership of a Resistance. It was good to know so many were prepared to stand up against the New Republic. Another man came up to say the packages were being delivered. When I asked what packages, the man looked at the Wall.

I knew immediately it was the explosives that Samuel was making and Lucas was distributing. The Grunts were filling holes in the Wall as they repaired them. Replacing the rubble with explosives and detonators was the prelude to making a new Unifying Event. The people were just waiting on my signal. I would have to make it a big one.

This new attitude and recognition were bound to spread to those I would wish instead to remain ignorant. Even as I adjusted my appearance, changed my routes, and staggered my escapades among the GP, I was being watched.

There was that itch at the back of my neck, warning me of eyes trailing my every step.

Ducking down an alley, I gained speed as I pushed past rubbish and the riffraff. More than I liked, I came across patrols of the Protectorate. When able, I slipped past without more than a suspicious glance. On a few occasions, I had to alter my appearance back to my own. A large crowd was being detained by a random search of homes, soldiers acting on a tip from a neighbor, someone wanting to garner favor by turning on one another.

I looked at a nearby GP woman hanging clothes to dry on a makeshift line. With a brief look back and a nod to the woman she knew I needed help.

As I ducked down another alley, the woman pushed over her baskets of clothes. They fell into the path of the man pursuing me.

I had no time to look back, but I could tell from his raised voice and use of language he was an Enforcer and not the grunt he made himself appear. I had to ditch my own disguise and blend back in with my given place among the Protectorate.

It took only a moment to switch back into my regular

appearance. With a swift turn of my cloak inside out and pulling out my lapels, I was MacKenzie Dillon, First Commander of the Protectorate. I slipped out from a doorway as a contingent of Enforcers walked by.

"What is your report here soldier," I said to a nearby man.

His face was hard as he turned, but recognition of his superior brought downcast eyes and a quick salute.

"We have the suspect in bondage and are now searching the residence for subversive materials, First Commander."

"As you were," I told him and began surveying the scene.

There were a fair number of soldiers present, far more than would typically be necessary for such a search and arrest. As I looked at the crowd, the itch returned. My pursuer was nearby and watching.

I scanned the onlookers and soldiers equally. In a time where everyone around you can not be trusted, I had to suspect any and all around me. No eyes met mine as I looked from every filth covered face of the Grunts to the clean and pristine among the Protectorate.

Making my way into the thick of the gathered force, I thought to surround myself with those sworn to serve my rank. I was greeted with a heavy mix of disdain and forced obedience. It was my upbringing and lack of parentage added to the accelerated and sudden rise in my station that made even the most conditioned of soldiers both envious and chary. I had to shove past a few men who waited too long to make way for their commander.

"What have you found inside?" I asked, forcing my authority. "You've been too long in finding proof of guilt."

Was it fear of failure or resentment of my position that made them pause? I think partially both made my men hesitate. When at last I received my answer, I had to make a decision on the spot.

"There is nothing found to support whatever claim was made against this man," I said. I pointed to the accused and watched his color return to his cheeks. "Release him immediately."

"But sir...I mean First Commander, there was accusation laid upon this man's character." A soldier said, his eyes did not focus upon mine.

"Accusation is not proof and guilt is not placed on those without proof of a crime." I began to fill with rage against the New Republic's ways. "I will not have my time wasted in higher court without just cause."

"But sir, the Edicts state that the accused must prove their innocence before-"

"I know the Edicts soldier," I interrupted. "You can not attach guilt without substantiating a claim. Release him and bring me the accuser."

I heard a throat clear behind me and turned to face the source of my irritating itch of watchful eyes.

"It was I who laid the claim," said a familiar face from my ranks. "I saw him passing out papers in the markets."

He was once my second in command—not long ago—and the resentment in his glare spoke volumes against my position. I only wished I remembered his name. I never formed bonds, never cared much to know those I served with or those who served me. Relationships were a weakness in an age where they quickly turned sour.

"Do you have one of these pamphlets?" I asked.

He faltered in his stance against me.

"I do not."

"Then my judgment stands. Release the accused and compensate him for troubling him."

"We have no recompense on hand sir," a soldier answered.

I turned to my former second. "Then give it to him from your personal credit."

I made my stalker an enemy.

I had little time for grumblings and turned away. I took note of the eyes now daring to meet mine. The gathered witnesses and neighbors of the acquitted were meeting my gaze with what passed as appreciation mixed with skepticism. I wondered what they made of their new First Protectorate Commander after witnessing something that had been missing for generations—just cause and due process.

I decided it best I made my exit and took the first lift I found back to another level. I did not go far however as I knew I'd be followed and didn't yet want to force the confrontation that was coming. I knew this man who followed my movements was not going to give up without seeing me executed, so I had to transfer his target for me onto his own back.

Chapter 22

After several detours and changes of level, I returned to my Grunt disguise and made my way through the markets until I felt my inner senses itching again. He was back on my trail, and this time I was going to make sure I led him on a merry chase.

I ducked through a market stall selling old rugs and dingy decorations salvaged from the Wastes. Technically these items were forbidden because of their link to the outside, but it was impossible to prove their origin as long as they were cleaned well.

I learned more about how well the black market ran through my new connections. This stall, as well as most, made their livelihoods from items reclaimed from the ruins outside the city. An entire network of smugglers worked the ways in and out of the city as well as the workers who mined the outside for diamonds and minerals released from the explosion of Yellowstone. They made the right bribes and paid off their Elite sponsors, but only for what they claimed.

Many objects from before the Unifying Event made their way this side of the wall daily. The soldiers who guarded the convoys, if not paid off, were either blind to the goings on of their charges, or just cared little to pay attention.

My attention was on making sure I could stay ahead of the man giving me chase. Now that I knew who he was, I had a small amount of satisfaction or at least I thought until I caught a glimpse of who was chasing me at that moment.

It was not my former second in command but rather a Grunt or at least someone made to look that way. I failed to think that this man might have a payroll of informants ready to turn in their own family. It was not unheard of to have a network of spies among the population. Many a wealthy man still grasping onto the material world through longevity treatments and medical advancements made their fortunes by underhanded means. A society could advance, growing in knowledge and science, but still fall short on the growth of humanity.

I made sure my tail was close enough to follow as I allowed myself the chase. I had to admit that I was now having fun ferreting out who else might be in the pocket of my rival. Though my former underling had little chance of usurping me while McCord was my sponsor, I could still enjoy plucking the leaves from his branch of spies.

With great purpose and direction, I made my way through familiar streets where I would pass those who knew my disguise. Members of the Resistance were many, and I began to recognize their gaze as I passed those who remembered my many faces. With a nod and glance back I was able to identify my need for assistance. All it took was the right look to a friend, a word or phrase in New

Polari, and those who chased me would be dealt with.

I only paused the first time to see how those who favored freedom and liberty dealt with traitors to their own Caste. My first of many leaves was plucked without mercy.

More people than I could count descended upon the man who gave me chase. The beating he received at the hand of those he would turn over to the Protectorate for credits was bloody and rage-filled. Hate and rage fall back harder on those who perpetrate than those who receive it without cause.

I had to turn away and continue my parade to draw out more leaves from the thorny branch that would present my true enemy bare and without cover.

One after the next, the network of spies set against me were exposed and dispatched with as much or more vengeance as the first. I did not abide such violence—usually—but in a world made to hate, sometimes what was required was a release toward a deserving target.

My attention was pulled away by the outrage and cries from a nearby automat. A reimagined relic of generations past, it was one of the ways the New Republic provided for its general public. It was a food distribution center. The more enterprising of the lowest caste built around such centers making the machines that spat out food. They were businesses for keeping folks around for trade and purchase the distilled spirits and have a gathering place that was not considered illegal.

Machines spat out artificially produced edibles that passed as meat and vegetables while the staff and owner of the pub made use of the device to create a more delicious menu. They were not allowed to charge credits for the food—directly—but could demand a service fee for the delivery of better meals with accompanying spirits. Booze loosened the virtual coin purse as quickly as it did tongues.

The source of the uproar that night was the broadcast of news that gave me the first clue as to what the real power in the New Republic was planning.

A reporter for the National News read from a statement provided by the Lord Chancellor's offices. There were reports of an attack being readied by the bordering nations in allegiance to the recently uncovered leaders of the Old Union on the western coast. Claims by the West that an attempt on the life of an Envoy led to the joining of forces to destroy the New Republic.

The reporter spoke the scripted words of how the rest of the world called the New Republic a shit-hole country not worth saving. The Lord Chancellor was not going to take such a threat lightly and was preparing a defense.

I knew immediately that this was all a lie and that the defense of the New Republic was a ruse to mount an offense. They were going to use the weapons provided by the Envoy against him along with Canada and Mexico.

The Lord Chancellor opened a new can of worms by admitting the survival of the Old Union in the west. Lies perpetrated over the last century and a half about nothing out in the Wastes but cold, snowy desolation and destruction were coming to light. To cover one lie with another was the standard operating procedure for the real rulers of the government. The wealthy and powerful would do whatever it took to tighten their grip on control.

"What has Canada and Mexico to do with this?" The crowd began murmuring. "They've historically been open to trading for essentials like food and water?"

"They have nothing to do with this!" I found myself shouting. "It's all lies to take control of their land and resources."

As the crowd turned toward my direction, I saw a face I hadn't expected. My former second was there in the pub. The man was taking a more personal approach to my entrapment than I expected. I supposed that since his spies were no longer…available, he had to come out of the shadows.

I was not prepared to reveal my disguise, though I had little doubt he knew exactly who I was. It was past time I left.

Jostling through the uproar of protest and debate in the pub, I pushed my way toward the back exit. I felt the brush of hands on my collar as I struggled through the people now arguing the truth against fake news.

It did not matter how bad their lives were or how little they had, far too many of the Grunts still clung to the bullshit spewed by the Lord Chancellor and his superiors over the ages. It was far easier to latch onto lies than truth. Honey-coated false words stuck to minds easier than the cold hard facts of reality.

His name was Handson, I remembered as I felt him right behind me. Another grab, and he had hold of my cloak. Pulling hard against the drag of my pursuer, I struggled and did not notice my lapel flip out to expose my rank pin. But someone in the crowd saw it clearly.

As Handson gained better hold and began to spin me around, someone from the crowd stepped between us and began battering Handson with questions and pushing him away.

"What are you doing in our pub Protectorate slime," the man said to Handson. "Bad enough you bastards entrap and abuse us on the regular, now you gotta come to our pitiful feeders and harass us?"

More enraged patrons descended on Handson, forcing him to call his hidden company in from the perimeter to assist. I just made out the smirk on my rescuers face as I slipped out the back. I did not know the man nor did I ever see him again, but his help made the difference that night.

Outside and free from the itching irritation of being followed, I made my way back to the city center in old New York. There was going to be repercussions for this close call, and I had to get ahead of it. I needed to find Tinker and Lucas.

Chapter 23

"Can you get it done?" I asked Tinker. "I have little chance of pulling this off if you and Lucas here can't do what I need."

"Don't you worry Mr. Mac," Lucas said with a wink. "I got this all wiped up and shiny for you. You can betcha me and my crew'll get the goods on that slimy Protectorate pants-crapper."

"Colorful kid," I said to Tinker. "How about you? Are you going to get that done?"

I looked down at the device Tinker was 'tinkering' with.

Without stopping his work, Tinker huffed and gave me a sideways smirk. "As the kid here says, don't worry."

I was worried as I left my hope of getting Handson off my back. My churning stomach found no relief as my summons came shortly after making it back to the nearest elevator stations.

"First Commander Dillon," the mirthless voice announced over my communicator. "You are expected in the chambers of Vice Chancellor Pincer without delay."

Just like that, my day went straight from hovering the toilet to deep in the shit-pit.

The Vice Chancellor held court in his chambers as he would in the main hall, highly formal and commanding. The man outreached his station as though he ran the entire world. Even then I suspected his connections were farther stretched than just the New Republic, but everyone reports to someone else, and I needed to hold my cards close before I could play against this sorry bastard.

"Commander," Pincer said. His voice was no more or less than even and yet carried more venom than usual. "It has been brought to my attention that you have been on patrols among the Grunts."

"I have taken to walking among the 'General Populous', Vice Chancellor."

The tightening of his eyelids spoke to the displeasure of being called out for using the derogatory term for the population.

"Yes. This is rather unusual behavior of a Prime Commander."

"Perhaps in the past, but I find that to control a people, you must first understand them."

"What's to understand? They are weak-minded masses of filthy people that-"

"That represents ninety-nine percent of population and entire work-force of New Republic. Without their obedience, we would be hard-pressed to survive as Nation." The interruption came from the First Lady.

I was shocked to hear anything but innuendo come from her lips, but I would soon find out there was more to the unfortunate woman than was being portrayed.

"Rightly so, Madam First Lady." Pincer begrudgingly agreed though I held no doubt it was for my benefit.

Regardless of the dynamic that existed between the First Lady and Vice Chancellor, I had to wonder why she was even in attendance.

"You have been called here for two reasons Commander. First is the accusation of inciting unrest among the General Population, which I am sure is without substance."

Reading between the lines was becoming far too easily done with this man. I was sure he was prepared to burn me at stake with whatever minuscule proof he might have from his witness. Handson was his little informant.

"And the second, sir?" I asked with as much dismissal of his first statement as possible.

"That is a matter for McCord to address."

As though on cue, McCord entered the chambers carrying a small box and a look of satisfaction mixed with worry.

"First Prime," I said and saluted McCord.

"Not exactly," McCord answered. "Not after today that is."

"I'm afraid I do not follow sir."

McCord gave me that knowing look that said you aren't going to like this and that he was putting more on my shoulders.

"I have been pressed into diplomatic duty," McCord said. He opened a box on the desk before us. "As such, this leaves my position as First Prime vacant, and it was agreed that since your harrowing acts surrounding the Envoy, you are best suited to take on the mantel."

McCord looked deeply into my eyes sharing his concern over the appointments for us both. Removing my former stripes of rank, he then turned me to the First Lady.

"It is my duty and honor to place insignia of First Prime upon your collar MacKenzie Dillon. Do you swear unquestioning loyalty to Chancellor and his house?"

I paused only a moment before answering. "I do."

Pornia gave my collar a quick tug and squinted at me slightly and meaningful. She wanted something from me. At least I had my answer as to why she was there; the ceremony to place my new rank and bear witness. That was half the reason. Her personal reason for being there was yet to be revealed.

"Now that that is out of the way, how do we deal with this accusation laid upon your feet First Prime?" Pincer asked.

More confident in the assurances of my rebel contacts than myself I turned to the Vice Chancellor.

"Let the accuser face me with proof."

***

There were three levels of court in the New Republic: Commerce, Enforcer, and Protectorate. As the previous First Commander, I presided over the Enforcer court's major cases. Commerce court cases were a matter for the wealthy men who owned everything and there appointed Justice. As First Prime, I would typically reside over the Protectorate courts, but since I was the object of accusation, McCord was appointed one last case.

Elite and Protectorate soldiers stood shoulder to shoulder in the court. There was room for a regular gathering of a hundred but was standing room only at over half as much more.

Protectorate soldiers both supporter and foe were in attendance to see what would happen. The Elite present always enjoyed watching their lessors under scrutiny they themselves avoided. Trials were a spectator sport for the bored wealthy and social climbers alike.

Commonly—as the accused—I would have been paraded in with armed soldiers and placed in the seat of burden. Instead, I walked in ahead of McCord and after the Vice Chancellor. The murmurs and hushed whispers echoed throughout the chambers as I took a seat beside McCord sitting at the head of the judgment bench.

McCord removed a large marble ball from a divot in the bench and knocked it on the table.

"As former First Prime, I take honor in residing over one last case before turning the task over to our newly appointed First Prime, MacKenzie Dillon seated beside me.

It is with great importance we dispatch with the unpleasantries of allegations against our First Prime in alleged actions taken while he served valiantly as our First Commander of the Protectorate."

Again the murmurs and exclamations rose in the crowd. The ordinary course is a burden of proof on the accused, but now that I claimed a position at the highest rank among the Protectorate, I garnered a portion of privilege reserved for the Elite. I was innocent unless irrefutable proof lay against me.

"Let the accuser be presented," McCord ordered and knocked the spherical gavel on the bench. "I'll have quiet and order in this court."

As the doors opened, I watched as all in attendance turned to see Handson stride into the room. His cockiness faded when he saw me seated on the bench, my new rank reflecting the lights into his eyes.

Though I noticed the boy disguised as an Elite child, Hanson failed to register the bumping as that boy passed and exited the court.

My faith in Lucas was strengthened as he winked and dashed out of sight. I don't know how that boy manages to get around, but he had his foot into more places than I suspect even Pincer had.

Handson came before the bench and was asked to present his

formal accusation. He looked from me to the Vice Chancellor, over to McCord and then back to me. Straightening his back, Handson moved his eyes to somewhere between us. He focused on the back wall, not knowing whom to address.

"I have come to express my findings to this court of the Protectorate. During my duties in service of the New Republic, I have witnessed the accused, Commander MacKenzie Dillon, in violation of the Edicts."

McCord looked at the formal charges displayed on his tablet before asking Handson to elaborate.

A long list of accounts was read from his statement, all but one being second or third-hand information. Only the reports of his personal witnessing were allowed in the court.

"Your use of information from the General Population is not admissible in this court," McCord said. "What first-hand knowledge and proof do you have with your claims?"

Handson turned his eyes on me and his brow furrowed as he glared. "I have seen this man, Commander Dillon, personally. I have witnessed him walking among the Grunts and fraternizing with them. He coddles and assists, using them for some unknown purpose."

McCord refrained from showing concern. "Commander Dillon, you have been accused of being a decent and fair caretaker for the General Population. How do you answer to this charge?"

I almost laughed. "I would be guilty if that were a crime, Your Honor."

"Just so. It is not a crime, but some would argue a part of the job. As to the second argument that you are in conspiratorial contact with any persons known or unknown to this court, how do you answer?"

"Contrary, Your Honor. I was in fact, adjusting my presence

among the GP to better garner trust and information for my own investigation."

When McCord asked me to what investigation I referred, I mentioned the use of banned foreign technology and collusion with another nation to inform on state secrets. The investigation led me to obtain the identity of the said individual who now stands before the court.

McCord shared a confused yet impressed look.

"Handson is here only as means of deflecting my investigation away from his person."

Handson began to cry out but halted at the sound of McCords gavel.

"What proof do you have for these accusations?" The Vice Chancellor said.

"Check his person, I believe he will have said device on him."

Handson stiffened with the shock of discovery, blinking the only movement he made as the guards withdrew holding the contraband device and presented it to the court.

Handson was immediately stripped of rank and charged with conspiracy against the Protectorate and fabrication of accusations to cover his treason.

Guilt soured my stomach, though my shoulders felt the weight lifted from my own stay of execution.

McCord made his final decree of judgment in the courtroom before turning the position of First Prime to me.

"As you have been found guilty of treason against your First Prime, you are sentenced to reconditioning which will be carried out immediately."

Handson was taken away and led to the transport bound for the space station. We were all going, and one above all else expressed his joy in what was to occur.

Pincer displayed what might pass as a smile. It was hard to tell with his face all pinched up always.

Chapter 24

Few individuals outside of the scientific branch of government were allowed to witness the advances and technological marvels whether reengineered from Space Force acquisitions or gained from foreign countries by other means than trade. It was all stolen when boiled down to simplest terms.

We boarded a transport for the space station. I wasn't pleased to be heading back there, but my new duty as First Prime would mean more time in space and access to secrets I later regretted knowing. Ignorance may be bliss to some, gaining knowledge of secrets and what truly transpires behind the scenes becomes seductively addictive.

The flight into space was not what I had any problem with. We took off with feeling only the slightest of change in pressure or movement thanks to the inertial dampening field. Even the close flyby of wind turbines, the massive blades spinning in the high altitude jet stream to create power for the upper levels of society, did not phase me. It was the transition through the ionosphere that gave me a chill every time of late.

"Something troubles you?" Pornia asked me in her broken English. "You should be used to transition to space by now."

I pinched the bridge of my nose and shook my head to clear my thoughts. Why was this woman even accompanying us? Aging a couple centuries never improved her grasp of the National Language. If she were not the First Lady, she would have ended up deported or banished.

"It isn't that," I admitted. "I just always have this odd feeling as we pass through the outer boundaries of the atmosphere. I'm not sure why."

I had not expected to gain attention from the Vice Chancellor, but Pincer showed a bit more interest in my revealing this fact.

"Describe the feeling," he demanded.

"Just a chill similar to what is described as someone walking over your grave." For some reason I did not experience the feeling this time.

"Such quaint and outdated concept," Pornia laughed. "Graves are thing of past I would say—at least for those who can afford longevity such as us."

"Yes, well graves are still a poor concept in theory," I said. "Except now they are more ash-pits where the un-useful remains of the condemned are interned after harvesting and incineration."

Pincer huffed and sat back. "I hope you haven't a problem with the processes that afford you the same longevity and luxuries your upbringing did not ensure."

There it was, the underlying problem that Pincer and all Elite had with me or others elevated to higher stations. We did not come from money and privilege. There were far too few of the Elite to fill every station in government, so some of us bottom dwellers were necessary. There was some semblance to ancient process of affirmative action. The Elite couldn't be bothered with the details of running the government, so they chose among the lower class. Grunts to do grunt work.

"I only feel that a bit more respect for the dead should be shown. After all, most of the population still live, serve, and die. Most of them continue to serve after death as spare parts for the rest of us."

Pincer was unmoved, Pornia, however, showed a slight bit of emotion, though it was difficult to tell with as tightly pulled as her face had become from surgeries and treatments. Fighting off the natural order of aging was a never-ending struggle once it started. I suppose I was lucky to receive my first longevity treatments at an early age. This poor cow had more wrinkles than a hairless cat when she first became extra-mortal. If she were pulled any further a bikini wax would include her chin.

"I imagine families of those who pass would agree with your assessment, First Prime," Pornia said. "Perhaps you might enact some measure of respect now that you have power."

I was under no illusion that I had any real power, not while her man-child husband sat as Lord and Master over his orange regime.

"Perhaps, My Lady, should the New Republic see fit to grant such changes." I looked directly at Pincer.

He shrugged. "Anything may be presented to the Lord Chancellor."

"He seems rather agreeable these days," Pornia said, her tone edged in optimism.

"Not for long," Pincer mumbled.

I expect I wasn't meant to hear that so I kept my eyes and

attention toward the viewport. I watched the builder-bots and drones outside the space station going about their programming of repairs and upgrades. The station was aging, but constant updates and patching of damage from micro-meteorites and space debris kept it operational. I glanced at the ring of space junk that spun around the planet like man-made rings around Saturn. Humanity found a way to trash up everywhere it went.

"We're here," Pincer announced. "Let's get to it shall we."

The prisoner was carried from the back of the transport and floated on a hover-gurney behind us. I heard him struggling when we first set off from the capital, but he quieted with a final cry. Seeing his clouded eyes and flaccid state, he was tranquilized heavily.

"He'll be revived for the procedure, not to worry," Pincer said. "Can't have a clouded mind when trying to rewrite it."

There was far too much mirth in his voice. The man was looking forward to the mental torture this poor guard was about to receive. I had no love for Handson, but he did serve me well as it suited him for a time. He set his own path though when deciding to go after me with blind envy.

Being present for the re-conditioning of the man was my right as the acquitted and as First Prime now. I had not expressed a desire to be there, but Pincer assured me there were others to attend. This meant there was someone with high standing that required my presence. I also needed to take occupation of my new office on the station.

"Welcome sir, First Prime," A station officer said. "We will settle you into your new office here on the station. If you need anything changed, please let your guards know, and we will take care of your requirements immediately."

The man turned and strode ahead without another word. Once

we made our way from the inner docking ring we were in the heart of the station. We walked through unfamiliar corridors and past all the laboratories I was previously too low-ranked to gain access.

I had no clue then as to what transpired in those rooms and still wish ignorance. The lengths to which people will go in the pursuit of power and eternal life never cease to astound me. Even if I still believed in GOD, I would say he or she or whatever order there is to the universe should not be tampered with.

Man is not meant to live forever, particularly if he is unable to learn from his own past. My mother used to paraphrase an old quote that history and experience are the best schools should the fools of the world care to learn from others rather than attend.

"Your office is within First Prime," a guard said when I was left behind by my previous escort. "We will remain here until called to bring you to witness the procedures."

The guard never looked at me. Yet another envious soldier or a mindless follower of the New Republic. I had to put aside such thoughts as I walked into my new office finding I had a guest waiting.

"Nathaniel?"

"Hello handsome," Nate said as he came before me and planted his warm moist lips firmly upon mine. He looked over my face and form. "The new rank suits you. I see your ugly scar has healed."

"What are you doing here?"

I looked at myself in a wall mirror. I hadn't even noticed the scar on my forehead was gone again that morning.

He laughed and turned toward my inner office. "I couldn't let you take this office the state it was in. McCord is nice enough, and all, but his taste in decor is simply the twenty-first century. I took the liberty to get assigned as your personal liaison to the Elite. With that comes certain responsibilities, least of which is making sure you are in every way presentable to the Upper Castes. Starting with this office." He then looked at me and tittered. "Then we need to address those clothes."

"What is wrong with my clothes? It's standard issue Protectorate garb."

"It belongs off your body and on the floor," He said and began to undress me.

Pushing him away with a reluctance that battled my resolve, I zipped my pants back up and went to my desk.

"As enticing as your deviant invitation is, this is neither the time nor place for illegal acts."

"Bah, you are practically Elite Caste yourself now. We can do practically whatever we want."

"The Edicts apply to all members of the New Republic so long as they exist."

Nate waved off my words as though I spoke gibberish. "Rules only apply to those lacking the influence to break them without repercussions. Do as I say and not as I do I think the saying goes."

"Nate, sometimes I feel as though I don't know you at all. Some rules may be bendable, but our relationship is a death sentence. Anyone who knows about us is a liability, and you might escape such a scandal, but I am not privilege-born."

"That's what we are trying to change, isn't it? Bring back the freedoms and principals of the old Constitution and ancient ways?"

"You mean freedoms and liberties? Yes, but we can't just cram things down people's throats."

"Oh, dirty talk!"

I had to push him away again. My resolve would crack and break apart if he kept touching me the way he did.

"Nate! I'm serious. You have no idea what it was like in the time of the Cleansing when people were rounded up and dispatched.

Worse was after the first exile of the undesirables. Far too many had no means of leaving the States or tried to blend in to stay with their families."

"What do you know of it Mac, You were just a kid then, and your conditioning did away with most of your early memories."

"Those memories were only buried. And I have since learned a great deal by second hand. Old news reports and being in that horrible place out in the Wastes."

I had to remind him of where I had been to take refuge from the cold and barren land where my escape pod crashed with the Envoy. The horrid outbuilding of a former containment camp. The stench that still lingered over the remains of gassed and burnt bodies of people deemed unsuitable for society when the New Republic began its bastard birth.

"It was horrible for you, I get that. You are here now, safe and able to begin working on change. Change doesn't happen in a day or a week, not without a Resistance and our own 'Unifying Event'."

"You need to stop talking," I said. It dawned on me that my office was likely peppered with surveillance.

"I already took care of the bugs," Nate said. "Give me a little credit."

"I give you too much credit."

"What is that supposed to mean?"

The sounding of my chamber bell announced someone waiting outside. "Saved by the bell."

I could hear Nate's eyes rolling from across the room at my use of 'ancient' phrases. I knew then he would be the death of me, just not when.

Chapter 25

My escort to the first of several demonstrations left me in the care of a lab tech who felt it necessary to speak down to me and describe every minutia of the mind control and conditioning procedure I was about to witness.

"I am well aware of how this works," I said. I was still agitated by Nathaniel. "Can we just get on with this, I have a great deal on my schedule for this evening."

I really had no clue what the rest of my evening had in store for me at that point, but why prolong the inevitable. A man was about to be erased and reprogrammed at my hands. I wasn't going to be performing the procedure, but my pre-planning made certain Handson was implicated where he would have seen me fall from ranks. Of course, I alleviated my self-deprecation by convincing myself the man placed himself in this predicament by envying my position, but that was semantics and only a contributing factor.

I set in motion the chain of events that got us to this place. I became a player in McCord's game. I allowed the Resistance into my daily activities. It was I who then set Tinker and Lucas to task on providing evidence against Handson.

Tinker duplicated that OU device and falsified the history of communications between Handson and a fabricated conspirator. Lucas then managed to acquire the clothing and access to play the part of an Elite child who was in the courtroom. I'm sure Tinker had to hold the kid down to bathe him first.

This allowed Lucas to plant the device on the man who brought accusations against me. My elaborate tale then had the support of laying fault on my accuser, thus vindicating me.

As the patient was rolled into the lab, strapped down and fully coherent, the bottom of my stomach threatened to squeeze everything out. He pleaded and screamed for mercy.

Too late were the lights in our booth dimmed. Handson denounced his accusations against me as he saw my face through the observation glass. Screams turned to muffled grumblings as an orderly placed a plastic guard into Handson's mouth. Though his vocal pleading was curtailed, his eyes spoke of his wish for retraction. Having already seen me in the booth, his gaze felt as though it saw through the two-way mirror and spotted mine in the concealed darkness.

"It is awful process, but results are worth suffering," Pornia said leaning to my ear.

"I very much doubt that without being conditioned to speak so, the patient would not agree to the worth of this act. It is merely a necessary evil."

"Rightly so," Pincer said. "I'm happy to hear you admit this Dillon. I was afraid you were not of the correct mindset for your new position."

"I do what is necessary Vice Chancellor. I do not have to always agree with the methods, merely the results."

"Well spoke," Pincer said with what might have passed for a slight smile of approval. "I think it a good idea then that you attend another important procedure this evening."

"I wasn't aware there were more conditioning procedures tonight."

"Not exactly."

I turned my attention away from the odd stare of Pincer and grimace of Pornia. For the present, I was holding back my disgust at the acts playing out in the chamber beyond the glass. Handson was strapped from shoulder to toe before the last restraint was used across his forehead pulling his head back and completely immobilizing him. I was expecting the use of a visual stimulant and accompanying headset, but something different was taking place.

Another white-coated medical tech entered the lab with a cart. The top shelf held a computer tablet along with a small vial and hypo-syringe. Taking the hypospray and filling it with the bottle, the tech then laid it upon the computer tablet and pressed the screen. From the lights emitted in the syringe, I could tell something within the fluid had been activated.

Nano-tech, I had heard rumors of it being tested and used for medical purposes, particularly around reversing the aging process. Now I was witnessing its latest application. Nano-devices programmed with specific instructions to aide and assist in the control of human thoughts and will. These were in that container from Minsk. The hairs on my neck stood as an uncontrolled shiver ran down my spine.

"You know what that is, First Prime?" Pincer asked.

"Nano-tech would be my guess."

"Such a primitive label. These latest devices are far more than those we use to iron our wrinkles and stiffen our dicks. This is autonomous biotech with an AI. It relays directly with our central computers and monitoring systems."

I watched Handson's veins bulge as the machine-containing liquid was shot into his system. As his eyes squeezed against the attack to his mind, his white-knuckled grip on the chair began to slack. Whatever this new means of control was doing to him, it was far faster than what I endured over years of conditioning. I was feeling nostalgic for the old ways of torture and control from generations before. I would not stand up against this type of conditioning if I were a young initiate in today's Protectorate.

"You see, once the devices have taken their places along the neural pathways, we will be able to monitor and predict everything this soldier thinks and wants to do before he knows himself." Pincer was enjoying the description of what his new toys could achieve. "If we do not like what we intercept, we simply change his mind, actions, disposition…we make him do whatever we want."

"A puppet then," I said without restraint.

Another laugh escaped the Vice Chancellor. "In a manner of speaking, I suppose yes. The Manchurian man for a new age."

As quickly as the thrashing of Handson began, it subsided and his eyes halted their darting around the room. His grip eased on the chair's arms, and he sat still, waiting.

The medical tech punched a few times on this tablet and nodded toward our presence on the other side of the mirror.

"All done." Pincer slapped his hands together. "Let's get on with the rest of our unpleasantness for the evening so I can get back to Earth. I do hate these space visits."

We walked out from behind our concealment and into the lab. As we passed Handson, signing our names to the witness forms and observing his new state of compliance, another shudder cascaded down my spine. There was a vacancy behind his eyes that stirred my resolve.

This man attempted to have the same thing ultimately done to me. He envied my position and advancement to the point of following me, discovering my duplicity and would have exposed me had I not turned the tables. Regardless of his actions against me and the position he placed me in, I did not wish this upon him. He was essentially erased. Now I had to go witness something worse performed on another.

As we migrated toward our next subject, I noticed the change in atmosphere and surroundings. The air was less stale, fresher such as the filtration reserved for the Elite classes on luxury ships and bases off-world. The lighting and decor along the corridor walls and ceiling also changed. We were in a diplomatic section of the space station.

My mind reeled at the thought of having some foreign diplomat on-board that the New Republic was planning on controlling. How did this poor bastard get caught up in such a devious plot, I wondered.

Pincer again seemed to read my thoughts.

"You are wondering who would be under our control from foreign nations?" Pincer asked.

"Yes actually," I admitted. "It would be the most likely scenario and probable use for such advancements."

Pincer just released that creepy little fucking laugh of his again. He was more than a little amused at witnessing the unraveling of New Republic secrets to a new initiate. That, and I felt he enjoyed observing and controlling the suffering of others. While still Vice President this man led much of the efforts to eradicate all remaining undesirables from the country. His primary target was the LGBTQ community, which he tortured and killed.

I had to force out the images of what lay in store for me when eventually Pincer found out that not only was I involved in treason against the Republic but also gender bent and involved ass-deep with the Resistance at that point. By the time I was over my head, it would be too late to reach my neck and slit my throat.

When we finally made it through the well-appointed corridors and into a regally decorated reception room, my attention was refocused on the insignia on the far wall. A golden Omega on a field of red, the flag was lit up from overhead lights making sure all in the room noticed the importance. This was a room reserved for the highest among the castes and known only to the few.

The Omega Caste was no longer a myth or rumor. I was being allowed the knowledge of their existence, but not yet who they were. Those who actually ruled and governed from the catwalk, pulling the strings of their puppet Chancellor. They were sending a message, and I was moments away from witnessing the truth of everything.

The wall where the Omega flag hung slid back and to the side, revealing another room within. It was a lab, but unlike the last, I visited. This lab was filled with Cryogenic chambers and computer screens. Only one technician was in attendance, busy prepping something on a table while another room opened before us. Laying within was the Chancellor, Lord Dampnut.

"What the fuck is going on?" I whispered.

"What has been going on since the beginning, First Prime," Pincer said with more satisfaction in his voice than I ever heard from him previously. "We need to make constant adjustments to our leader's personality—until recently that is. With our latest breakthrough, this should be the last time we need to reroute this imbecile's thought patterns."

"I'm not sure I follow, Vice Chancellor."

"My husband, the Lord Chancellor," Pornia started, "has been in state of deterioration since before he was elected President of then United States. Medications helped to slow progression of his demented mind, but when person's ego far out-sizes their capacity for rational thought, there is little medication can do."

So I learned that the leader of the New Republic has been controlled not only by the financial backing he received his entire life, but now I found out he was actually controlled through mental conditioning. He was about to get another round of conditioning, only this looked more sinister than Handson's.

The lab tech turned and approached the cryotube that housed Dampnut. He carried a large pair of forceps holding a two-inch long—thing—in the end. The device looked to be a tiny mechanical centipede with small lights at the end of each leg. A high-pitched squeal emitted from the device as it was placed near Dampnut's ear.

"No more!" Dampnut pleaded. "It hurts me."

Pornia shushed her husband, though the look in her eyes held no remorse or concern for the man. I could only imagine how empty her heart was of any regard for the vile pig that he was. Then again I felt little regard for her as a mail-order whore that allowed herself be bought for a life of money and American citizenship. She got what she deserved as many thought over the generations. I was conflicted, feeling that nobody ever deserved being treated as property and just another pussy to grab.

Seeing the weak-minded dribbling fool in the tube, however, I felt only a stirring of regret for what he was being subjected to. He willfully destroyed America and made hate a part of the status quo. He pandered to the most basic of human emotions to rise to power and once in, unwittingly allowed himself be used to push the

Omega agenda.

Then the squawking centipede was released into Dampnut's ear.

The skin rippled on my arm in rhythm to the screams that came from Dampnut. The chorus reverberated in the chamber. As I took a step back from the tube, Pincer pushed me back into eye-shot of the torture transpiring before us. Dampnut thrashed and wailed, breaking his arm in the process as it pulled free of a strap. When at last the man settled and was getting his arm repaired by a medical machine, I was free to step away.

I turned only a moment to see the screens light up around the room, relaying everything going on inside the Lord Chancellor's mind. I joked to myself how surprising that any activity was registered in his brain, but even an ego-maniacal sexist idiot has the most basic of brain waves. Dampnut sat up and looked around the room as though someone else was using his eyes.

"Back to business," Dampnut said. "Is this our new First Prime then?"

I approached and saluted the Lord Chancellor. "Greetings and allegiance, Lord Chancellor."

"No need for all that crap in here, young man. We don't hold to all the ceremony and stuff we show the grunts." Dampnut took my hand in his. "Welcome to the club."

"Club sir?" I said.

"Have you not been briefed?" Dampnut looked at Pincer. "Get him one of those old-time folders with the secret seal thingy on it. We have the best secrets and seals. Nobody keeps secrets like we do."

Nope, I thought; still the same moron, just more pliable.

"I'll send over the dossiers via electronic message to your office, Dillon. For now, you are dismissed." Pincer waved me off.

Pornia and Pincer stayed behind as the Omega wall closed

behind me. McCord was sitting in the room waiting for me when I turned to get as far away from there as possible—while on a space station orbiting the planet.

Chapter 26

"What the fuck did I just witness?" I said to McCord.

His face registered no surprise at my reaction, he spoke Polari to me due to surveillance.

"Mince bencove, we nights palare here."

He wanted us to walk. As we left the room, McCord motioned away my questions, letting me know that we could not speak freely. The journey back to my new office passed slower than I had hoped while my agitation and concern boiled over.

Once back in my office, McCord poured two glasses of whiskey, making mine heavier after I gave him a look of needing it.

"You'll read more details on what you just saw in the reports Pincer will be sending to you as well as the classified documents to which you now have clearance. That said, let me fill in some highlights."

The tale was long and full of more reasons to hate what the world had become. From the end times of the United States, when the states were trying to secede, and the government threatened to impeach Dampnut, backup plans were set in motion. It started with the Unifying Event as a means of preventing impeachment and elections. Martial law was implemented, keeping the puppet leader in power.

The Omega, the wealthiest men in the United States and a few men outside the country wanted absolute power, and Dampnut filled the role of catalyst perfectly. For his part, it was easy to feed the ego of the pseudo-celebrity and pampered rich jackass, getting him to follow most of the orders given. So long as he was the center of everything, Dampnut did everything asked. But then he began going off-script and ultimately had a meltdown that ended with the explosion of the supervolcano.

"That wasn't part of the plans, but there were contingencies, and under martial law, the Omega could begin taking more drastic actions. They wanted things simpler and streamlined, and ultimately they wanted a country of old rich white men controlling everything."

"It isn't enough though is it?" I asked, already knowing the answer.

"No. Dampnut has been out of the public eye as much as possible for decades due to descent into full dementia."

"He's a babbling halfwit."

"Yes well, not anymore. That thing they placed in Dampnut's head will give full control of his mind and body to the Omega. And they plan to use him fully to begin an offense on the rest of the planet."

"Fuck. The United Nations won't stand for that. They'll launch against the New Republic."

"They won't be able to. Contingencies are always being planned, and the Omega has their fingers in every pie around the world. There will be no counter-strike capabilities."

"What?"

Then McCord laid out the full story behind my reason for being conscripted into his service. I was chosen based on a genetic marker making me suited to help overthrow the system. McCord knew I would overcome the early form of conditioning. McCord knew how to break the mental deformity placed upon my psyche. He and his cohorts knew what situations to place me in and what triggers to use. Triggers that somehow broke the conditioning that made me agree with the regime of hate that became the New Republic. I was also a puppet, but my strings were now snipped.

"Your parents—like so many—were foolish enough to send away for one of those family ancestry kits. Those ridiculous tests were highly inaccurate histories, offered to get as much DNA profiling of the nation as possible." McCord sounded as though he admired the long-laid plans of the Omega. "They played the long game. Plans laid out for many decades, and then they let them unfold through the use of a fluke that got an idiot seated in the highest office of the country."

I had some genetic quirk in my make-up that would allow me to be programmed but only so long as I was not subjected to the right mix of events. McCord was part of all this. He knew who I was and what role I would play because he was part of a faction that did not wholly agree with the Omega plans.

"I was and am part of that group, but I never agreed to the full plan of dominance," McCord admitted. "We used you as our backdoor."

So I was chosen by a part of the Omega to take down the rest of them. I had a difficult time processing everything McCord spat at me until he took out an OU device.

McCord laid an identical communication device like the one I had on the table. He described how he planned for me to find the one I got, arranged for Eli to meet me and just how far-reaching this subterfuge reached. Eli was also a member of the Omega, though he was also part of the Old Union.

"Did you really think that the survival of the OU happened without the knowledge and approval of the New Republic. Where do you think the new technologies were developed? The morons that make up our population are not smart enough to see what they started by supporting Dampnut in the first place. Those with the intellectual wherewithal to even think for themselves are not here. We have traded our forcefully taken tech through Space Force and allowed the OU to adapt it for our purposes."

Not only were the Omega not satisfied with taking over our own planet, now preparing to launch missiles against the world, but they've also been making enemies across the galaxy as well by stealing technology. So the "Greedy Rich American" way still seemed to live on into the current regime. First, the world came to hate America and then the New Republic. Now Earth would be shunned by the entire galaxy unless they already saw us as just a shit-hole planet.

My head was pounding from information overload. Granted I already knew a small degree of how the world was reshaped and half destroyed so that those with power could take control, but to put all the pieces together and find that even those who once were part of the plans had bailed…How worse was it expected to become?

"We have to stop this now Dillon. It has gone too far for even the majority of the Omega, though none of us dare speak against the master plan. None of us even know who more than a few others are among our ranks."

"The Missiles and strike against our neighbors would be a good place to start then," I said. "How do we stop this?"

"You are now in a position to do something about a great many things, least of which is getting whatever Eli needs to counteract the nano-tech."

The attack planned was not another means of destroying more of the planet and limited resources. The world was still struggling to recover from the effects of Yellowstone. So the new offensive was to introduce the mind-altering technology into the atmosphere.

"That shipment container from the Envoy, that is where this tech originated? Why would Eli deliver such tech?"

The OU device McCord presented emitted a comm beep.

"Yes I delivered it, but the Omega faction controlling the New Republic have perverted the tech."

The voice came from the OU device on the table. It was Eli Minsk.

"They have reprogrammed the devices to reproduce themselves and restructure into that mechanical bug you witnessed being implanted into Dampnut."

"And you can't stop your own creation?" I asked.

I had little use for Minsk, particularly knowing now he was a member of the Omega and using me just as McCord was.

"This is fucked up, you know that right? What about contingencies? You spoke of the long-game and the Omega having all these plans and counter-plans."

There were plans, but neither Minsk nor McCord would share them all. What they did share was the need to acquire the altered tech. We needed a sample set of the nano-bots and the new code to develop countermeasures. My sudden rise through the ranks finally started making more sense. McCord chose me precisely because I broke my mental conditioning as he knew I would. But there was more to my being selected.

"Your DNA profile not only makes you the prime candidate to thwart this nasty business," Eli said, "but may make you immune to it. Part of the reason Pincer hasn't had you killed yet. We had the foresight to know where many of our paths would lead, but not always the detours. The Omega makes plans within plans with a great deal of flexibility, but this time, there is little room for missteps. And we are not as sharing of information among our own as we once were."

A division of power began decades previously. The Omega Caste started breaking into factions, each with their own subset of plans and agendas. These agendas began to alter and split from the rest of the factions. Now, though the richest and wealthiest in the World still controlled everything, they did so without unity or cooperation. To get back on track to the ultimate goal, full control over the global economy and resources, the Omega top ranks were prepared to use this biotech to alter the minds of the entire planet.

"If you are unable to get what we need in time, then we have to move against the delivery systems themselves and sabotage the missile launches," said McCord.

"That will be far more difficult than stealing some samples and the base code," Eli said. "But it wouldn't be that hard to delay things a bit. I can have a program whipped up from my end that will cause some disruption in the guidance systems and pre-launch checks."

I was not a code monkey, so I had little faith in myself at working on hacking the systems of a Protectorate controlled space station. But I knew someone who was well adapted to 'tinkering' with technology. I trusted Tinker more than Eli.

Chapter 27

I had to think of the best way to get Tinker onto the station. He was far too old to pass as a Protectorate soldier and as adept as Tinker was with technology, he was the polar opposite when it came to dealing with people. Posing as a commissioned officer was also out of the question as anyone who was old and in power was also very well known after having lived for generations with longevity treatments. Grunts did not have any bio-markers for longevity and would not pass a scan. There was only one way we could get him into space, as a prisoner.

"Nope!" Tinker shouted. "First you want to get me off the ground and onto that infernal tin can in the vacuum of space. Now you say I have to be a prisoner to boot. You're a special kind of ass-jockey MacKenzie Dillon."

"Tinker, if there were any other way, I'd be open to hearing it, but I can't think of any other means of getting you up there."

Nathaniel plopped down on the couch next to me with a look that betrayed his thoughts. He knew of another option but was reluctant to speak when I prodded him. I knew he was hiding something because he was silent. The only thing Nate enjoyed as much as sex was talking, sometimes at the same time.

"Spit it out Nate," I said. "What has your tongue stuck to your teeth?"

After a few seconds of half-hearted denial, Nate gave in. Of course, I gave him that look I know he melts for and he called 'bedroom eyes'. His weakness for old phrases and dead languages was a bit annoying at times, but I used whatever I had available.

"Fine, but you can not—under any pressure or torture—reveal this to anyone. I have not gotten the commerce patent release yet."

"Just get to the point fancy pants," Tinker said. "You know I mean that in the most loving way."

Nate waved off the joking insult and explained his little venture. "Avatars."

"You mean like in the VR suites or Holo-games?" Lucas asked. "How are we going to use virtual surrogate bodies to get onto the space station?"

"Not a game, and not virtual," Nate said. "Real, live, human, avatar bodies."

"You have the tech to take control of other people?" Tinker said with a mix of horror and curiosity.

We all looked at Nate with a bit more shock and repulsion. Considering the nano-tech we were about to risk everything to stop, and he already was using something similar.

"No, I may be a bit self-serving and flighty from time to time, but I would never subvert someone's freedom of thought. It's one of the few freedoms we still have."

"Too bad more grunts don't use that freedom," Tinker said. "Seems to me that's how the world ended up in this state of Trumpery. Idiots who chose not to think for themselves put that puppet of the Oligarchy into power."

"Though that is in part true," I started, "It would have been another puppet eventually had it not been Dampnut."

"As I was saying," Nate said.

Nate cleared his throat to return our attention to himself. Center stage and all eyes on him, just the way Nate liked. Nathaniel explained his invention and how it worked.

Bodies were manufactured using biotech much like that used for tissue regeneration and longevity treatments. A cybernetic and lymphatic system controlled basic survival systems, and synthetic blood carried the necessary nutrients and fluids throughout the body. What Nate created was nothing short of a computerized body that only needed a driver.

"How long?" I asked.

"They have a special battery system that constantly recharges as the avatar is in motion—even breathing. The avatars could essentially last indefinitely."

"That isn't what I'm asking. How long ago did you start using these avatars?"

Sheepish grin followed by a defiant sneer told me all I needed. I wondered how Nate could go so long.

"Wait," Tinker said. "They breath?"

These avatars were nothing short of a mindless person functioning on auto-pilot to live. They needed all the same things to live as a normal human, so they breathed and took in nutrients.

"So if they eat—they shit," Lucas snickered. "What does robot shit even look like?"

"Lucas, they only release waste if waste is taken in. When I use an avatar I generally only ingest nutrient-rich supplements that release over time. The system is still computer controlled for the most part, so efficiency is controlled far better than the normal human body."

Nate pulled up a portfolio of his current sampling of avatars. Most were variations of himself, cloned from his own DNA, but there were others that looked familiar.

"You aren't the only one with access to the DNA profiles of every New Republic citizen," Nate explained. "I can fabricate a replica of anyone from the Elite to second level Protectorate goon."

"Let's get moving then. I don't yet know when this missile strike is scheduled, so we need to move fast."

After we arrived at my transport, I activated the system cloaking device Tinker gave me. We didn't want anyone tracking us, nor did I need internal scans of my vessel revealing my passengers at that point.

I tried talking to Nate on the trip to his facility, but he was a bit dismissive and distracted. He made apologies and excuses about coordinating what needed doing in preparation for our arrival. I knew Nate, better than I felt he knew himself. Something else was bothering him.

Our flight to Miami was quick and without impediment. Once we landed and made our way through his apartments and into his secret laboratory, Nate loosened up some. He looked around for something he didn't find, which seemed to ease his mind.

"You were expecting Protectorate soldiers to greet us?" I asked.

"No, they do not know of this place. It's heavily shielded, and the original plans for this building were lost long before the fall of democracy."

"Then what was bothering you?"

"Nothing...I am just concerned with my secrets being

revealed."

"What other secrets have you not shared with me?" I asked, half playing.

Part of me knew there was something he was keeping from me. Something far more important and damaging than this laboratory, and his living doll collection.

"These self-replicating and collective processing nano-bots, they have capabilities I would bet credits on that came from this lab."

"You think someone stole your tech?"

"It's a possibility, but more like they were appropriated."

From Nate's description of his security, it was far superior to that of the Protectorate systems or those of Space Force Station. His only deduction was that somehow he was scanned at some point in his escapades out in an avatar. There are a few things that could interfere with the avatar self-shielding systems that would allow a scan. One of those is systems that existed only in his own laboratory or electronic interference like that experienced traversing the ionosphere.

"Have you ever gone into space in an avatar?" I asked.

"A few times. I'm not concerned about the several seconds in transit between the atmosphere and space. You'd have to be actively looking for something in narrowband to pick up anything. Even then it would take multiple passes to get enough to reassemble any useful code. The system security would reactivate as soon as the transition ended."

The way he looked at me was confusing at the time. I felt dirty for a moment as though he suspected me of something.

"Let's get to work," Nate said with a peck on my cheek. "Come along boys, let's get you sorted out with one of my studs!"

Dozens of cases lined both sides of the warehouse-sized laboratory, each containing one of Nate's avatars. His living dolls.

The implications of this technology were far-reaching. In cases of appropriate application, these avatars could be used for performing hazardous tasks or other situations where human life could be protected from risk. The far end of the fulcrum was the ability to impersonate anyone from whom you had DNA samples.

"How do you get past the ID chips?" Tinker asked.

"That was the easy part. Those in the avatar act as a direct relay to those of the actor, except the added bonus of using the avatar's DNA profile. So they register as valid chips."

Nate explained that sometimes the more difficult you make breaking security sometimes you leave yourself open to simple hacking. Then again the writers of the original security protocols on the ID system were not likely thinking ahead to DNA replica avatars...or were they?

Tinker was first to choose his vessel for operation "Nono-Nano" as Lucas labeled it. Tinker picked out a hearty-looking young man of apparent mid-twenties in age. Appearances though are deceiving when technology and medicine allowed those with means to live a very long time. Not to mention the advancements in youth extending surgeries has come a long way since the time I was an actual child. Images of scary-looking big-lipped celebrities who couldn't blink anymore came to mind.

Some of Nate's technicians began prepping Tinker for the transition to mind-controlling the avatar. While they dealt with his fussing and slapping away of hands, Nate and I walked with Lucas since he took more care in choosing a 'ride'. He was far more excited with the prospect of taking a different body out for a test drive. When Lucas finally settled on choosing it was between two candidates.

"So do I go with buff and dumb looking, or slim and...still dumb-looking. They are Protectorate soldiers after all."

"Go with what you know, the slim one," Nate said. "You would have difficulty adapting to a bulkier body."

Nate described how it is not at all like driving a vehicle or even controlling a VR character. When you took control of an avatar, you became them. Your instinctual impulses for breathing, walking, mannerisms, even scratching your ass became a natural and subconscious action.

"You have to remember though that you are not...you," Nate explained. "Your natural predilections and mannerisms will want to continue as normal, so you have to be diligent in not getting too comfortable in your new skin."

Now that both Tinker and Lucas were ready to undergo the transition to an avatar I began looking around at the others. Quite an assortment and more than a few replicas of Nate himself. I wondered what would require the man to use an avatar of himself. What on Earth did Nate get up to that he would be concerned about his safety? He noticed me browsing.

"Looking to upgrade me already?" He joked. "We could have some fun...another time though."

"That is not what I was thinking." Though now that he mentioned the idea, it did stir some sexual curiosities. "Anyway, what about me? Can we whip up a Dillon suit for me to use?"

"No," Nate was quick to answer. "What I mean is that you are going to be needed in the highest security areas of the station. The systems there would reveal you as a clone before the sensors recognized the low frequencies emitted that track back to here."

I could not argue Nate's logic, but I knew there was more to that quick denial. The silence that hung between us was relieved by the lab techs saying that Tinker and Lucas were ready for the transition.

"So you will be only lightly sedated enough to make the

transition between your own body and the avatar easier." The tech said. "Think of it as going to sleep in this body and waking up in the other."

Nate eased their apprehensions. "You will not actually transfer anything to the avatar, but you will feel as though you are outside your own body and for a few moments there will be a slightly disoriented feeling."

"The important thing is to allow your own muscle memory and natural movements to flow into the avatar." The tech said as Lucas and Tinker drifted between self and avatar. "Don't force anything."

Lucas's avatar opened his eyes and coughed on the first few words. "Don't force what?" As he tried to stand, Lucas tripped over his avatar's feet and fell flat on his face.

"You break it you buy it!" Nate joked. "We'll have to fix that nose before we leave."

Chapter 28

It would have been more amusing an adventure, watching Lucas and Tinker acclimate to their avatars, had the gravity of our mission not weighed on us so heavy. Lucas managed to stop tripping over his feet and became more than a little engaged with his adult-sized penis.

"Would you stop playing with it Lucas," I teased. "You'll grow into your own one day if you're lucky."

Tinker laughed. "I understand the preoccupation. I have to admit I'm enjoying a day off from my wrinkled old nut-sack hanging down to my thighs."

"That must be horrible for you," Nate said. "Everyday I find out more about how deplorable life is for the ninety-nine percent."

"Oh yes, the saggy-balls epidemic has surpassed a lack of nutrition and clean water." Tinker's words cut through to Nate's heart. "Sorry, I know you mean well, but you just don't know what it's like at all for those of us who live and die naturally, while the Elite stand upon our backs. We labor for their benefit until we are dust in an ash-pit."

"I am sorry. And you are right. Perhaps when this is all over, you can help me understand it better. Then I can get a real idea of what I can do to help."

Nate was sincere, and both Lucas and Tinker appreciated it, but they had no illusion that Nate would ever understand fully what life was like for the Grunts. He would have to live their life.

"Perhaps we trade places for a while, using these avatars?" Tinker suggested. "You could market your man-dolls as a break from civility for the pampered and spoiled of the Elite Caste. You think you have it bad, live a day in the life of a Grunt."

"As sarcastic as is your proposal Tinker," Nate said, "it isn't such a bad idea. You could create a mandate as First Prime, Mac."

"One treasonous act at a time if you please."

The mood lightened in time for the passage through the ionosphere. I was ready for the odd sensation I always felt. When my three companions also visibly shuddered, I knew there was a connection. I just couldn't nail it down. Nate said it could be anything from the avatars to the id chip implanted in us all. Nothing to worry about.

Nate placed a small device behind my ear. It was a secure communication relay that linked me to the avatars he and the others were using. We would need to stay in constant communication while I set up the other required relays for Tinker to work. Lucas was going to act as lookout and pass-off for the samples I stole from the lab.

Nate had his own reasons for coming along. Besides wanting to keep an eye on his avatars, he also wanted to trace his computer code. If it was modified for use in the nano-bots, then he might be able to identify how it was acquired. It was also fun for him.

The pampered and spoiled wealthy experienced a downside to the long-life that the workers like me did not. They did not work, not real work. So they got bored quickly. With travel to most countries out of the question for members of the New Republic, there was little to see within the confines of our walled-off nation.

Most of the cities were filthy pits at the ground levels and just like any other at the upper levels. Open land was used for farms, factories, or mining what little natural resources and water remained below ground. There were a few resorts and getaways for the rich, but they too were boring after a decade of visiting the same places.

Those of us that lived longer lives in service to the Protectorate had to always work, and vacations would mean something that cost little to no credits. No national parks or recreational land existed, so it meant going to the coast and hunting mutated seashells among the garbage strew beaches. I tried fishing once but only caught a cold.

The long-lived will never appreciate anything because there is a stretched sense of lifetime. How does one learn to cherish something if you can't think of it as ending? Perhaps that is why I allowed myself to be conditioned so easily. I felt that my life would be a never-ending routine of hatred and lies in the service of the New Republic. I looked at Nate, smiling and talking about the intrigue of sneaking around the space station, I found another reason to think differently.

I nearly missed my landing while not paying attention. We landed within the inner docking platforms of the station and made our way out with only a few soldiers stopping to salute. No one questioned my presence or the company I kept.

Being First Prime came with freedom of movement and unquestioned presence to which I was unaccustomed. More than a few times Nate had to calm me with a few words of reminder as to who I was to the soldiers and workers on the station. I was in charge. Even the Space Force answered to me while on the station.

"How are you speaking without moving your lips," Lucas asked.

'Talk inside your head,' Nate responded. 'It's like an inner monologue, except the avatars are equipped with a comm device like that I put behind Mac's ear.'

'What if the communications are intercepted?' Tinker said. 'We'll be shot out an airlock.'

"Keep quiet unless necessary," Nate whispered. "A little static on this frequency is normal and ignored, too much, and it will draw attention."

We proceeded to my office without further words. Once there, I set up Tinker with direct access to my terminal and left Lucas to guard the door.

Nate and I headed toward the development and research wing. Once we arrived, Nate was gone.

'Where are you, Nathaniel?'

'Checking on my intellectual property. Just get the bots and set up the relay for Tinker.'

Soon enough, I found myself in the finely appointed corridors of the Omega section of the station. It was labeled as the Diplomatic Wing, but I knew better after my indoctrination to the inner circle of knowledge. How a hall could be both richly decorated and still feel as sterile as an operating theater, I couldn't say. I was glad to have my back to it as I entered the Development and Research labs.

I was fortunate to stumble upon the plans for this section of the station, now that I had access. This afforded me the knowledge of how to locate the room where the nano-bots were stored. I did not have to enter through the secret panel in the Omega Chamber.

Having only been there one time yet, I was unaccustomed to the lack of activity. I saw only a few labs occupied by technicians as I moved around without much notice. Being the First Prime meant that I was expected to be anywhere I chose. When I found the lab where Dampnut was implanted with the control bots, it was empty.

The doors slid open as I stepped close enough. The system recognized my authority and disengaged the security protocols. As I stepped inside, I felt a cold chill.

The room was more than just sterile and still. Beneath my feet, the station's rotation could be felt through my thick-soled boots. The thrumming came from mechanics that kept the artificial gravity and geo-synchronized orbit stabilized. Normal operations throughout the station usually prevented one from noticing this, and the fact I sensed the motion added to my edgy nerves.

I moved toward a control panel that looked like what Tinker described as linked to the nano-bots systems. Reaching into my jacket, I pulled out one of the relays and began to place it on the console.

"First Prime," a voice came from the doorway. "Is there something I can help you with?"

I fought the urge to turn around.

"No."

I moved my hand below the console table and affixed the relay. Slow and without urgency, I began pushing buttons to bring up images on a display screen.

"If I knew what you were looking for, I might speed you along, Sir."

"I don't know what I'm looking for. Just getting to know what I don't know."

It was a vague and honest response. I had to play off my presence. I had no idea how much time McCord spent in these sections of the station before my appointment. Perhaps this was normal, maybe it was a surprise. I had to believe my presence would not draw suspicion.

"Very well, Sir. I will be in the adjacent lab should you find a need for assistance."

Once the tech was well away, I contacted Tinker to ask if he was getting what he needed. The relay was functioning but was not as fast as Tinker had hoped. Interference from the security systems and the placement of the relay were not optimal. When I tried to move the relay, it would not release.

'You'll have to disengage the security protocols then,' Tinker said inside my head. 'Otherwise, we will not have time to get what we need before the breach is noticed.'

'And how the hell do I do that?'

'Give me a minute.'

While Tinker did what Tinker does, I made my way to a cabinet that held vials of the nano-bots. It was locked, and my presence did not release the security. I looked around for anything that might help open the door when I found a hypospray on a nearby tray. There was a vial already inside the device, ready for administering.

'I have it,' Tinker said. 'What you need to do-'

I looked up at the sound of swishing doors and saw a reflection in the glass cabinet. I pocketed the hypo and vial as I turned.

'Out of time Tinker,' I said.

"First Prime," The soldier said from the doorway. "You need to come with us."

Chapter 29

I did not recognize the uniform, but the symbol on the soldiers' collars told me who they reported to. An Omega pin was affixed to the red collars of their dark-blue doublets. They moved through the corridors with all the authority of the ruling caste.

A new section of the station was my destination, the private chambers of the Lord Chancellor and First Lady. I expected I would be the guest of the Vice Chancellor, so was surprised by the sight of the self-appointed Lord Damp-pants and his mail-order bride.

"I hear you've been making your presence known in your new rank as First Prime," Dampnut said. "It's good to make people see your authority over them."

"I only wish to know what I am expected to oversee. I will earn respect as I go along."

"Respect is as fake as news," Dampnut said. "People will respect you for results and results will come from doing the right thing. You want to do the right thing I bet—be a team player?"

"Of course my Lord."

"Call me Ronald in private, Mackinny."

"It's MacKenzie, Sir…I mean Ronald."

"You know what I mean. Anyway, as a team player, I need you to do something for me. You want to make your Lord Chancellor happy and do a favor for the greatest man to be born, I'm sure."

The man just went on for several minutes, toting his greatness and accolading himself over all the 'Great and Important' work he's been doing for the New Republic and the world for decades.

"We finally got that wall thanks to me. So some government workers lost jobs and housing from not getting paid, that was poor financial planning on their parts. It all worked out for me in the end."

I had to stand there and listen to his dribble about himself until he eventually got to a point.

"Now that I'm feeling better. You know I have been a little under the weather, tired from all the stress of running the greatest country in the world. I made this country great you know, through all the good and right things I started."

"Yes, you started a great many things," I said.

I couldn't help saying it, but I noticed he wasn't even listening to me. I was just another follower in his presence and expected to be hanging on his every word.

"It has come to our attention that there is a bit of a ruckus among the Grunts. They seem to forget their place and level of intelligence."

"I'm not sure I follow sir. The citizenry of the General Caste is under control."

Dampnut pulled a flyer out from his desk and pushed it toward where I now sat. It was the flyer I had taken from my first raid months earlier. I would have thought it only another copy of the same propaganda, but it had the same smug on the right corner. Somehow this was removed from my possession and made its way to the Chancellor.

"The source of this material was stopped and his residence cleared."

"The Grunts are like a virus, MacKinny. They spread and fester if not completely irradiated on the spot. I need you to take a different approach than your predecessor McCord."

McCord's name he remembered.

"And what approach is that?"

"I want examples made. Start with some open and public executions, torture, whatever you find that creates fear and thus respect for the New Republic."

I sat there looking for an explanation of what I was just ordered. This mad man wanted me to start killing anyone that spoke out against him.

All the while that Dampnut spat his vile and hate-filled rhetoric, Pornia stood behind him as an obedient and loyal dog might stay near its master. Her eyes only met mine once but turned away when the Chancellor reached over and grabbed her privates.

"You can go now, First Prime," Dampnut said and dismissed me. "And take my bitch with you. Seems she needs a personal guard to keep other dogs from sniffing her pussy. See to it."

***

"That man is not Lord Chancellor," Pornia said as we walked the corridors.

"Are you saying he's changed since that thing was placed in his head? I would think that better for the New Republic than the afflicted mind he exhibited previously."

"I'm saying he isn't man I married all those decades ago. Don't get me wrong, I didn't like him anymore then than I do now. At least simple-minded pig can be trained. Whoever is inside his head now is not Lord Dampnut."

I didn't know what to say to her. I remained silent as we strode along the corridors leading to her chambers. Besides there being too many ears to hear our conversation, I was not prepared for another test of loyalty from the First Lady. My mind was on completing what we came onboard to accomplish.

'Lucas,' I said using that inside voice. 'I will be approaching you shortly. I need you to intercept me clumsily and retrieve the sample from my right coat pocket.'

'Then what?'

'Get it to my transport and then get back to your post. Once Tinker is done we need to get out of here.'

'Tinker,' I said. 'Where are you with hacking the launch systems and nano-code?'

'I have the launch system ready. Once they start pre-launch checks the virus will activate and send back false data. They will see everything as ready while the missiles remain in standby. The nano-code is a problem. There is some sort of added interference.'

When I tried reaching Tinker for details, there was no response. I could not reach anyone through the internal comms. As I approached Lucas, he shook his head slightly, indicating he didn't know what was going on, but he took the samples and headed toward the docking bay.

I could not risk stopping in my office with the First Lady in tow since I had no idea at that point where her affiliations lay. She may be truthful in her statements about the Chancellor, but that did not make me believe she was sympathetic to the Resistance.

I left the Protectorate wing behind along with Tinker to sort himself out. There was still no word from or sign of Nate so I had to assume he was doing his own thing and would turn up when it was time to leave.

"I'm just up here," Pornia said. "You might wonder why my chambers are so far from diplomatic section."

Not really, I thought.

I didn't care in the least. I just wanted to be rid of the woman. There had to be a better use of the First Prime's time than babysitting the First Lady.

"Well, it's because I'm only symbol to Lord Chancellor's appearance. He cares less for me than he does his supporters. I am possession and nothing more—old toy that he just can't seem to throw away, but with which he no longer cares to play."

"I am sorry for you First Lady," I said as I stood outside her door.

"Please come in and talk and call me Pornia please."

"I am unaccustomed to familiarity with the Elite Caste, let alone the First Family of the New Republic. I also think it highly inappropriate for me to enter your chambers unaccompanied."

"What I have to say cannot be heard by his spies, Mr. Dillon."

I really did not have time for this. "I'm sure that-"

Pornia pulled me inside her chambers and closed the door. She placed her finger on my lips and made a shush face while removing a device from between her breasts. She pulled me further into the receiving room before activating the small cylindrical device.

"We can speak freely within small a radius of this gizmo Jonny give to me."

She was referring to McCord. Things started to make sense for a second before my ideas of what was going on around me began to unravel.

Pornia told me of her affair with McCord and how it suddenly became an issue with the Lord Chancellor. For the past thirty years, the two had been together in private and were planning on escaping the New Republic together once Pincer was stopped. Then the Vice Chancellor ruined their decades of planning by having the nano-bots developed and implanted in her husband.

"He always knew about the affair, just not with whom. Once he or rather whoever controls him regained access to all of Ronald's memories, things changed. Suddenly the station went on alert, and all communications started getting monitored. Then Pincer came in today and dragged me to the Chancellor's office and had you summoned. Before you arrived, Pincer left to detain Jonny and capture some unauthorized new arrivals."

Chapter 30

"Shit...double shit," I said.

I was shouting in my head for Lucas, Tinker, and Nate. No answer. I tried my mobile comm device to connect to my office, but nobody was there. We'd been set up.

"I need to get out of here now."

"Take me with you," Pornia said. "I'll make it worth your effort."

Even if I had a carnal desire for a woman, it would not have been this woman. Though she was attractive in her artificially kept up appearance, I still knew her real age and background. The woman repulsed me, and she was the very symbol of inequity I despised within the New Republic.

"Not interested lady."

"I don't mean with sex, Dillon. I know your proclivity toward the boys. I mean resources, credits-."

"You have nothing I can't get for myself."

Pornia smirked at me, and the light in her eyes changed. She acted the fool but was not one. Her thick accent fell away.

"Men of power and greed have always dismissed the women they toss around like playthings. They think us intellectually inferior and weak, but that is their own weakness in understanding the drive that has always made women their superiors. They fear us, so they tear us down. I have the most powerful thing to wield against them should I choose the right soldier as my weapon bearer."

"And what is that?"

"Their secrets. Men run their mouths and brag among their contemporaries about conquests and deeds, they forget the women in the room. Men speak to impress the females they seek to dominate, thinking they lure us with the bragging and the sharing of their accomplishments. All they accomplish is giving us 'weak and feeble' women the tools with which to take them down."

She was right. She knew my secret, for all the good it would do her. I already had a sense my time was limited.

"If you can get to my shuttle, I'll take you out of here should I make it there myself, but that is the most I can promise. I can't guarantee anything now that my companions are likely taken and the knowledge of my duality gained. I need to get back to the lab."

"What of your friends and Jonny?"

"My friends will have to abandon their hosts. I need to make sure what I came for was accomplished. If not I will have to adapt my plan."

"Go to Jonny in the prisoner section. He will know what to do. Let me take care of what you need from the lab."

I argued for a moment, but then saw the logic in her idea. I began to trust her in so far as she needed me to get her off the station and away from Dampnut. So I sent her off with instructions on getting another sample of the nano-tech. I headed for lock-up.

**

It was far more challenging to find my way to the prisoner holding area of the station now that I had to avoid being seen. I had the schematics, so I knew where the cameras were and how to avoid regular patrols. The problem was that the regular patrols were now suspended and a search in progress. If they already had Tinker that meant Lucas, Nate and myself were also targeted.

The first group of Enforcers I came upon were lingering outside a lab. I ducked into a small supply closet. Opening the door an inch, I looked out to watch the guards split up and head in different directions. Two of them were directed toward me. I stepped back from the sliver of light coming through the cracked door. As each step drummed nearer, I thought of pushing the door closed, but dared not. I didn't want the sudden movement or click from the door getting their attention.

I held my breath as the men stopped outside the door. They talked about junk pulled from the debris field having a dead body from a failed space launch of another country.

"More like it was an enemy vessel attempting to attack or spy on the New Republic," The first man said. "We must have blown that foreign scum up."

"Or they just don't have good technology. We have the best space tech. The Lord Dampnut says so."

'Idiots,' I thought, still holding my breath.

They spoke for several minutes, hanging out in front of my hiding place. It felt like an eternity as I began thinking of nothing more than refilling my lungs.

"We better get back to finding those traitors," The other Enforcer said as they headed away.

They said traitors, plural, so I wasn't the last of my party. I let my lungs relax and refill, taking no notice at the time how effortlessly I began breathing again. As a young cadet, I remembered feeling the fire of my lungs while pressured to hold my breath during training exercises. This time I felt nothing, not even dizzy.

I eased from the closet and headed the opposite direction of the two guards. I had to make my way to a utility grate three corridors away. When I arrived, I found a guard standing near and blocking my way. I couldn't go back the way I came, because another two guards were approaching from the opposite direction. No closet, but there was a lab.

I entered the lab and found a technician coat. I put the jacket on and checked myself in the mirror. The coat was a bit snug, but it would have to do. Using a bit of my street disguise tech, I altered my appearance a bit. I rechecked my reflection then looked down at my feet. Though the pants were passable, the military style boots would be a giveaway. I had to play the odds that the guard was as thick as the Great Wall.

I waited for the other guards to pass. They looked at me through the lab window and nodded.

From the waist up and through the glass I was good, I thought. So I headed to the other door of the lab, it exited across from the guard.

As I walked out from the lab, the guard took little notice of me until I stepped nearer. He looked at me and frowned, then looked down. My boots. Before the guard could raise the alarm, I swung him about and wrapped my arm around his neck from behind. As I choked the consciousness from the man, I dragged him back into the lab and dumped him in the back. There was nothing around to tie him up with so I had to hope he'd be out long enough. Long enough for what I didn't know as I was making shit up as I went.

I dumped the lab coat and headed back to the hall. The way was clear, so I pulled the grating up from the floor and jumped down. I heard footsteps as I began pulling the grate back in place from below. I pushed myself as far into the shadows as possible while the men walked over my position.

The way through the utility service tubes was tight in a few spots. I had to lay flat and inch my way through twice before making it to my destination. I was right below the feet of a sleeping guard in the prison block.

I pushed up the grate as slow and quiet as I could. The steel grate creaked as it moved on the floor, disturbing the guard. A snort and cough were all that came out as he returned to sleep.

I slid past the sleeping guard and found my way to the cell holding McCord. The man was beaten and bleeding.

"McCord."

I shook his shoulders and lifted his head.

His eyes opened and focused on me. His wits returned as he looked around and then at the door.

"What are you doing here?"

"Getting you out."

Gratitude was not something the upper-crust was ever good at expressing. The military leaders were equally disadvantaged at showing any thanks. Two strikes against McCord.

"You need to get out of here Mac, there is no time for this. Get that sample out one way or another. Nothing else matters."

"They beat you senseless," I said. "I have already spoken to Pornia. She is on her way to get another sample from the lab and head to the shuttle."

"What? You can't trust that bitch."

Now I was confused. I told McCord of my conversation with his mistress and the plan to get another sample of nano-bots since the first was likely compromised. When I mentioned how the station was on alert for intruders and that Lucas and Tinker were already probably captured. McCord just stared at me blankly.

I shook his shoulders again before the door opened behind me.

"Well this saves us some trouble," The guard said. "Toss these two in with the 'First Prime' and McCord. I'll advise the Vice Chancellor."

Two more guards appeared and threw an unconscious soldier into the cell. It was Lucas's avatar. There was another prisoner, Pornia.

I caught her before she landed on top of me. After helping her to a bench, she told me how she was apprehended shortly after meeting up with Lucas at the shuttle. She sat next to McCord and began stroking his unresponsive face.

"Oh, my poor Jonny. What have they done to him?"

"Beat him senseless from the look of him," I said.

"Where did they catch you?" I asked. "Did you get to the lab?"

"I got to the lab okay, Just a bit of trouble with a lab tech. Good thing they didn't know about the guards looking for me. I flirted with the man, and while he was looking at my breasts, I pocketed a vial."

She told me how she then made her way to the shuttle, stopping only to wait for passing guards and stow the vial in a better hiding place.

"Lucas was there when I arrived at the shuttle. I told him about our plan for escape, and he played dumb for a few minutes before I told him about Tinker and Nate and McCord and everything. He really is but a child as you described, but very crafty."

Lucas was able to evade the guards that showed up shortly after Pornia met him at the shuttle. The two made their way only a short distance before they were cornered. When the guards took them, Lucas fainted and had been out cold since.

"He is not out cold," I said as I examined the avatar. "He's gone."

"What? He just died?"

"No time to explain," I said and dropped hold of the avatar soldier, letting him fall unceremoniously to the floor.

Pornia gasped at how I disregarded my friend. I didn't have time to explain, but I raised my opinion of the woman after seeing she retained a soul after all the years of surgeries and treatments.

"What happened with the sample of the nanotech?"

She didn't know anything about the hypo that Lucas had. The sample that Pornia managed to get was gone. She had it on her, hidden in a place she thought they would not search, but they snatched it from her, and it broke when a clumsy and careless second guard dropped the vial.

I had to figure out how to get out and back to the lab again. If we could make it to the lab, I would think then how best to get off the station. One problem at a time I felt as the recognizable boot clomping of a guard drew near.

The officer who entered the room winked at me just before knocking me out with an electric baton.

Chapter 31

I woke up in the lab where Dampnut was implanted with the mind-controlling nano-bug. The view of the room was surreal from the patient end of things. I had not noticed before, the mirrored ceiling. It was another level of torture. There was no purpose to the reflection of the room to anyone but the one strapped to the chair. I had to watch every preparatory step in what was about to happen.

I was going to be implanted with the new conditioning tech. All the strides I made toward recovery were going to be lost. I tried to fight my restraints, thinking about going back to a mindless tool for the Protectorate and the New Republic. I battle against the possibility of returning to being a torturer of the people and against of the evil that filled our leadership.

I thought of Nate and what I would lose. Would I remember him and if so, would I turn on him. The New Republic would have all the information in my head about the Resistance and those outside the Wall helping them. We were going to fail before the resistance even got started.

"I'm afraid your attempt to remove New Republic property from this station has failed, First Prime." The voice of the Vice Chancellor echoed through the room. "It was doomed before it even started, this little plan of yours."

"I don't know what you are talking about," I said. "I wasn't here to steal-"

"Lying is unbecoming a Protectorate Soldier," another voice said.

I recognized the voice, but it didn't inflect the same as it once did. Handson came into my view.

"Your plot to steal this nano-tech and provide it to the United Nations was shared with us before you, and your party arrived. Did you think that the New Republic and the technology of this station would not sense the arrival of clone cybernetics? Come now Mac, you're smarter than that."

Pincer lauded his knowledge of the entire plan from the moment we started landing. He already suspected my treachery and was prepared to stop us immediately. Then he had word from the Lord Chancellor to allow the events to unfold. Dampnut wanted to know exactly what we were doing.

It was Dampnut who allowed the subterfuge to continue as long as it did. He ordered the guards to allow us to sneak past. They were well aware of our positions the entire time. They had a way to track us even while my lapel pin was activated. I looked at my pin.

"That altered pin of yours will no longer work Mr. Dillon," Pincer said. "It hasn't since we saw the internals of McCord's after it broke during his...questioning. Once we knew what it was, our internal scanners were adjusted to compensate."

Pincer questioned me about my plans for the nano-tech before it was taken back. He wanted to know who was behind the failed attempt. He assumed the United Nations sent in a covert spy, the Russians most likely.

"They're still pissed off over an ancient misdealing for an apartment."

"I was not stealing the tech for them," I said. "I don't even know any Russians."

"Liar," Pincer said. He punched me in the gut. "Give him the centibot."

Pincer moved his face close to mine. "I call it that because it is artificially sentient and looks like a centipede."

"How original and well thought," I said.

He hit me again. "You will be screaming a different song soon enough, Dillon. I already own you, now I will control you completely."

"You will never control me, Pincer. I will find a way to fight this just as I did the conditioning of the Protectorate."

"That was child's play," Pincer laughed. "Compared to this new toy of mine, your first conditioning was a pinprick. It was only a small wedge that blocked your free-thinking and questioning. The centibot will link me to your mind and give me access to all of your secrets."

I felt failure filling my head. Waves of defeat carried the dead bodies of all my friends and contacts in the Resistance onto the shores of the New Republic. Pincer would know about the Resistance if he didn't already. He would hunt them down and replace them with avatars or worse, use me to do it for him.

I saw myself locked behind a two-way mirror in my mind, unable to fight the control of this evil man. There I would be, screaming inside my own head and helpless to stop myself as I watched and felt the atrocities I would soon be committing. I replayed all the horrific acts I already participated in before I broke the first conditioning. Those acts were nothing compared to what Pincer would force me to do.

Handson returned holding one of the bots in a pair of forceps.

The centibot screeched that teeth-grinding sound as it wiggled for freedom. The lights on the ends of its legs flashed in sequence to the rolling wave of their artificial limbs. I could already feel those legs creeping through my ear and into my head.

I was torn between thoughts of that thing burrowing into my head and the fact Handson was reconditioned as a lab tech. There was no background I could recall for Handson having education in technology. He was wholly programmed or controlled by another with those capabilities.

Pincer stepped back as Handson leaned in and hovered too close for my comfort. The spicy mix of clove and vanilla wafted into my nose.

"Just go with it and fake compliance, Mac," Handson whispered. "These won't have any effect on you. Except it will hurt like a bitch."

It wasn't Handson at all. It was Nate talking to me using Handson's body, another avatar. When did he have time to find cologne during all this, I thought. The rest of us were out sneaking and stealing and getting beaten while he shops and switches bodies. And where did he get an avatar of Handson?

The pinch in my ear preceded the screams I released as the creature burrowed its way past my eardrum. Then the lights began to flash, and I was suddenly not in the lab anymore.

I had a vision of the inside of a glass container and felt the suffocating closeness of a coffin. Light flashed before my eyes and shadowy tubes obscured my vision. Just before my eyesight cleared,

I was back in the lab.

The mirrored ceiling began to crack. After a piece fell and sliced into a guard, everyone in the room began to scatter. I was stuck in the chair and eyeing the ceiling. Pieces of mirror started falling along with the lighting as the supports shook.

Handson approached me and began unfastening my restrains. My head was free and first hand nearly finished when Handson slumped over and onto my chest. A piece of mirror protruded from the back of his skull.

I squirmed beneath the weight of the disabled avatar trying to pull my hand the rest of the way to freedom from the loosened restraint. I watched above as the shards of mirrored glass began to drop. Down a piece came and sliced through my coat sleeve as my arm was freed and I turned.

I pushed the avatar off of me and grabbed the mirror fragment wedged in the gurney where my shoulder once rested. I used it to cut the remaining bonds from my other arm and legs.

"Dillon," Pornia cried. "Help me."

I looked where her voice came from. She was being held by a guard and trapped in a corner by fallen debris. The guard was dead, several shards of glass protruding from him. His grip did not weaken from the First Lady.

I ran to her and managed to get Pronia free, but more glass was falling so we dove under a table. I took a moment to look around and observed the faces of the others in the room.

Pincer was gone. All that remained was a few guards and two lab technicians. The others were wounded or laying dead on the floor.

"We have to get out of here," Pornia said.

"Help me move the table. Unlock those wheels."

Using the table as a shield against the falling glass, we rolled our way toward the door. A guard tried to join us beneath our protected escape vehicle. Pornia took off her high heel and jabbed him in the eye. Falling glass finished him off.

We were out of the worst and near the door when I helped Pornia out into the hall. As I pushed myself free and headed toward the First Lady, I was hit from behind.

A lab tech managed to follow us and used a metal tray in an attempt to subdue me. I yanked the tray from the tech's hands and prepared to hit him back when a beam from the ceiling did the deed. The squish of his body flattened to the floor is a sound I'll not quickly forget. The crunch of bones accompanying the sound of a tomato being stepped on is the closest I can compare.

My head rang and ached from the tray hitting me. I turned to steady myself as Pornia helped me begin a retreat from the lab. The pain subsided, and my hearing returned. The hallway was clear of guards, the emergency alarms sounded, and lighting turned red in the corridors.

I heard arguing and saw lights flashing again. More than just the systems in the lab were malfunctioning. Something or someone was sabotaging the station. Tinker.

Chapter 32

Free from the chaos of the lab I looked at other rooms as we walked. The lights around us flashed, and display screens blanked out inside the rooms. As the technicians scrambled to regain control of their computers, I righted myself from Pronia's support and continued our unblocked escape. That is until Pincer turned the corner in front of us. He was accompanied by six guards.

Beside a small pinching behind my eyes and a slightly disconnected feeling, I felt well and prepared to run. Then I remembered Nate's words from Handson's mouth telling me to play along.

"What is your allegiance soldier," Pincer shouted at me. "Who do you serve?"

"I serve the New Republic."

I still don't know if that was the correct answer, but it sufficed at the time.

Pincer walked around me, his hot and rank breath curling the small hairs on my neck. As he looked into my eyes, I could only imagine what he was thinking. Then I saw a moment of doubt in his glare. He was standing up to me just in the presence of his guards.

I pushed back my shoulders and began to return his gaze.

"What are your orders, Vice Chancellor?"

Pincer stepped back, and the smallest twitch in his scrunched up face showed me that he might be believing my act. He turned to his guards and began to walk away. He turned back toward me, and I thought the play was over.

"Find out what is happening to this station and put a stop to it."

That was my cue to leave. I had an excellent idea what was happening to the station and wasn't looking to stick around and find out what else was planned beside the light show. Tinker had a flair for the dramatic.

"I'm coming with you," Pornia shouted.

I forgot she was with me. She had ducked around some debris when Pincer first came into view. Pincer didn't know she ran out with me from the lab and never took notice of her hiding poorly behind a failed beam. She credited being a woman.

"Being ignored has its advantages."

I wasn't convinced he had not noticed her, mainly because he went off the other direction. Granted he had no use for her, but I would think that there would have been some contingent of soldiers to look for the First Lady or others wounded in the lab.

"We must go get Jonny now and leave," Pornia said.

We ran through the corridors, lights flashing and coming loose from the ceiling. This was more than a slight hack job into the systems. Tinker outdid himself. As I thought about him, his voice sounded over my regular comm device.

"Hey First Prime asshat," Tinker said. "I might have gone a bit too far with my tinkering."

Running and dodging, I just skidded past a falling fixture. "You think?"

"Long story short, I was in your office enjoying some chocolates and whiskey that were just begging for me to eat them…you know real chocolate tastes so much better than the synthetic garbage we get ground-side."

"Focus Tinker, I don't have a lot of time here."

"Anyway—like I was saying—I found my way into the main systems and sort of destabilized the orbital programming. So basically, you are headed into the atmosphere."

"So then we can just leave and let the missiles burn up in re-entry along with the station," I said.

"That's not a good idea for two reasons. One, the missiles are set to launch before the station reentry would destroy them."

"And number two?" I asked.

"A station of this size will not break up enough in the atmosphere to avoid causing catastrophic damage. The current trajectory would take this thing down right on top of Eastern Europe."

"So we need to stabilize this place?"

"Too late for that. We need to blow the hell outta this tin can and soon. I'm working on it."

"Great, get back to me with ideas."

"Oh, speaking of number two," Tinker added. "It would be a good idea not to go back to your office."

"Why?"

"Just before I left the avatar and came back Earthside I had a bit of a scare from some guards bursting in."

"And?"

"Well, it seems brandy and chocolates don't agree with an avatar's waste management systems."

Still an image that's burnt into my mind.

We had to fight our way back to the brig. Even in the chaos of a malfunctioning space station, many of the guards still clung to the idea the Lord Chancellor would save them. Several others however, ran at the first sign of trouble.

The first two guards we took out, me with a roundhouse kick and Pronia with a leg to the groin, provided us with pulse pistols. The guns allowed us the humanity of only stunning the next few men, rather than kill them. I didn't want to kill any of those who were not aware of the false faith they carried for our leaders and the Protectorate. They would have to choose a side soon enough if and when the truth was shared.

No more guards were around barring our way. A few guards walked along corridors, and we ducked aside to allow them to pass. When we made it to the brig, McCord was still in the cell attended by the sleeping guard.

McCord was still sitting on the bench in a catatonic state when we entered. It took the effort of both myself and Pornia to drag him out of the cell. We barely made any progress toward the center of the station where the shuttle was docked. Two Enforcers blocked our path.

I let go of McCord who began to stir. As I approached the Enforcers, they pulled their shock batons and readied to attack. When I got close enough to see them better in the flashing of lights and smoke, I saw the image of Nate on one of their faces.

The Nate avatar deployed a full charge of electric shock into the other Enforcer's neck. He dropped on the spot.

"What are you waiting for gramps? Let's go."

"Lucas," I said. "What are you doing in Nate?"

"Um, it's not like that pal," Lucas said.

"You know what I mean."

The floor shook beneath us again.

"Never mind that now. Help me with McCord."

"I'm coming," McCord said.

He was unsteady at first, but McCord managed to move along with us as we tried to make our way to the shuttle bay. He was slowing us, but I would not leave him behind. He pressured us to leave him only once, but a smack from Pornia and hard 'not happening', stopped him repeating the suggestion.

The station felt like it was stabilizing a bit, but it was just the first wave. Tinker assured me that more shaking and destabilization was on the way. He was in the systems and following what the station command was doing to try and counter the virus Eli provided. Every step they took to bypass the damaged systems, the virus backtracked and undid their work. Though they had some control at that moment. Tinker relayed that the virus was working toward a full shutdown soon.

Tinker came back on my comm device and told me that we only had about half an hour before the entire station entered the atmosphere. By then we would have to be clear of the docking bays, or we wouldn't make it out.

"The station seems stable enough now Tinker," I said. "I can still get to the missiles."

"No, you can't," McCord said. "They are on a weapons unit that is outside the station. You'd have to be in a shuttle or space suit on the outer hull to reach them."

"Don't worry about the missiles, Dillon," Tinker said. "I should be through the firewalls protecting the guidance systems and launch protocols any minute."

"Then why mess with the orbital systems?"

"That was all thanks to Eli's virus. It had more subroutines than he told us," Tinker said.

I tried to reach him again, but the comm went dead. Eli Minsk was putting us all at further risk, again.

We began walking faster until we were running. McCord was having a hard time of it. He didn't seem out of breath or weakened, but the wounds on his head were deep and probably caused internal damage. From the way he moved, he was favoring his right side. Though there were no visible wounds, that didn't mean there was nothing wrong.

The Enforcers were taught many ways of torturing without leaving marks.

"You need to get off this station," McCord said as he stopped running.

"We are all leaving now," I said.

"No, I am not going anywhere," McCord held his hand out.

I moved to argue but didn't get the chance.

"None of you are going anywhere."

That was all I heard before electricity burst through me and darkness that followed the lights flashing in my eyes, ended my consciousness.

Chapter 33

I opened my eyes to have the pinched-up face of the Vice Chancellor staring into mine. His hot and pungent breath offended my nose hairs.

"Back away thee Satan," I said. "Have you been licking the Chancellor's ass?"

Pincer pulled back and swung his hand at my face. I expected a hard blow to the head, but there was little weight or power behind his child-like smack.

"Wow, I'd say you hit like a girl, but that would be an insult to the likes of the First Lady. I've seen how she can pack a punch."

"Thank you," Pornia said. "I'd be happy to punch out his lights."

Pincer turned on Pornia and slapped her.

"Oh, you do hit like a girl!" Pornia said.

She spat her dark blood out at his feet.

Pincer stepped back and pulled out a weapon. He aimed it directly at Pornia.

"It would seem nobody on this station is of use to the Omega any longer. So many fake people."

Pincer pulled the trigger and blew a hole directly through Pornia's head, spraying grey matter and dark fluids on my face and clothes.

As I pulled a cloth from my jacket to wipe my face, I looked around the room. Trophies lined the walls and shelves. Everything from antique guns and swords to stuffed animal heads and pictures of Dampnut with various people of importance—the Omega most likely. I tried to get better looks at the faces but was stopped by an Enforcer's grip on my shoulder. My gaze lingered on the Hollywood star hanging on the wall behind Lord Dampnut.

"You see all my prizes," Dampnut said. "I have earned all the trophies—great trophies. Nobody has trophies like me."

He looked at me and spoke of his great worth and wealth. Bragging about himself was never a complicated process no matter how delusional he became. The bloated self-image seemed to weather the passage between states of idiocy and dementia. There was a change in the man since earlier in the day. His lucidness was waning.

"You didn't come from the right family, McKinny."

"MacKenzie," I corrected.

"Nothing was ever good enough for you people. Not enough rights, too much taxation, I can't marry who I want. Blah, blah, blah. It really is sad, so sad. We had the best country in the world before the lib-tards started whining and listening to the people. Pushing fake news about global warming and dirty water. Meanwhile, our country was being overrun by brownies from the south and Muslims from the Middle-East.

Nobody cared about the jobs that those people were taking. Nobody cared about the security of our borders. I had to shut down the government, and people still didn't listen. Then those left-wing nut jobs tried to have me removed from power. Well, I taught them. I showed them all. I got my wall after all didn't I?"

"You had to blow up a volcano to do it," I said.

"Doesn't matter. It unified my people, my supporters. My approval rating was higher than anyone ever. I still have the highest approval rating. A record."

"That is the real fake news. You alter everything that is allowed through the media."

"No, we only tell what needs to be said in a way you puppets will understand. You see you are all here to serve and play a part. And you play that part well. All my little puppets."

Dampnut looked at Pornia. "She is a puppet."

He looked at McCord. "He's a puppet."

"You are just another puppet McKinny."

"MacKenzie," I said.

"Doesn't matter. You aren't able to understand the position and power or great responsibility that I have. We need to have more, always more and the best. We have the best of everything."

I stopped paying attention, noticing the Vice Chancellor pinching the bridge of his nose. Then Dampnut got personal.

"You were just a peon Grunt—worthless—when the enforcers came and took you. Your DNA showed promise for conditioning as a soldier, even though it also showed the gender-bent deformity you would likely exhibit. What was that old chant the Enforcers would say?"

"Better turnt than burnt," Pincer said. "Either the fags were fixed through conversion, or they were burned in chambers with the rest of the trash."

"So you turnt, then turnt back again," Dampnut said. He waved at an Enforcer by the door. "Bring in that pansy...the Walters' wasted spawn."

Dampnut looked at me.

"You are a product of that Muslim fake President in office before me," Dampnut said. "There was a time I thought we got rid of all you queers along with the retards, jews, lib-tards, and spics—all the Jesus haters and undesirables were gone. Then there were the genes we altered and fixed, but I guess sometimes a bad fruit finds its way back into the bowl."

Nate was dragged in by the neck. I tried to move toward him, but the guard holding my shoulders, pushed me back down. I looked at Nate—knowing—he just winked and looked up at Dampnut.

"Do your worst, you fat deranged imbecile. You still shitting your pants like an elderly toddler, Damp-pants?"

"Very sad for your parents. I know them. Terrific people the Walters, all those stores. Someone will have to tell them of course, about their disease-ridden son."

"The only one here with a disease is you, fat orange bastard. Look at you. You sit there like an obese half-witted monkey on a branch picking your nose and ready to fling shit from your diaper."

The Lord Chancellor stood up and waddled his way to the side of his desk. Reaching out toward the wall he pulled down a sword. The weight and size of the weapon came crashing to the credenza, shattering the glass top. Dampnut kept his grip on the relic and dragged it until the end hit the floor.

Without a word of warning or moronic response, Dampnut lifted the blade with both hands on the hilt. Putting his considerable weight behind the thrust, Dampnut drove the edge through Nate's back, severing the spine. Liquid spilled from the avatar's mouth. The artificial blood had a distinct reddish-black color.

Nate's avatar's head fell to the floor. His lifeless stare drilled into my heart. I knew it wasn't him, a replicant made to serve as a stand-in and put in harm's way. That did not stop me from feeling a loss and experiencing the pain for a moment as though it were real.

Those feelings turned sour and vengeful. That this slug of a human being would feel nothing for another. That life was worth less than the trophies that adorned Dampnut's walls—it was reprehensible.

Even the Enforcers that held me were stunned enough to loosen their grip.

I pulled free and reached toward the sword, but Dampnut pulled it back, slicing my hand, leaving a dark fluid running loose from the wound. Dampnut slammed the sword down without looking. It now rested in the abdomen of his lifeless wife.

Dampnut looked down at the remains of Pornia. For a moment he looked as though he would cry, but stopped and looked at Pincer.

"Why did you have to go and ruin another one?"

"Oh shut up already Dampnut," Pincer said. "An all-time record with how quickly new technology lost the battle to control your weak and smooth brain."

"Damien, why are you here anyway. Shouldn't you be shooting my missiles at the bad guys? Bad—very bad—those people."

Pincer looked up and leveled his weapon on the Ruler of the New Republic.

"I've had my fill of you."

Pincer shot the Lord Chancellor in the center of the chest, dropping him on the spot.

That moment, the station alarms sounded again as the structure began to shake.

"I've been waiting over a century to do that," Pincer laughed.

Pincer stood there, smiling over the dead Chancellor, his blood pooling on the floor. The thought of Pincer taking full control of the New Republic made my skin crawl. I thought the climate controls in the room shut down as it felt like the room filled with a skin blistering cold.

"You won't get away with this Pincer," I said. "Assassinating the Chancellor to take over won't work."

"Oh, that isn't what I'm doing you fool. We have planned for this day and have the means to replace him with a clone."

All this time, I began to wonder, Dampnut has been a puppet for the Omega in more than just taking orders. They had Nate's technology and would just replace him with another given a chance.

"Now you begin to see," Pincer said. He waived a data disk in front of me. "With these upgraded specs, we can replace anyone, anywhere, at anytime."

I was preparing to lunge at Pincer when the floor beneath us began to shift. The station was moving.

"Time to go."

Pincer left us there, me and McCord, surrounded by the lifeless remains of two avatars and the bloated body of the man who sat at the head of our country for over one hundred and fifty years.

The floor beneath us shifted and the gravity lessened for long enough to lift and drop us back down a foot.

"We need to go," McCord said.

I nodded but looked back at Nate's body. I closed the eyes of his avatar and did the same for Pornia. Reaching over I took possession of the ornamental sword the Lord Chancellor used to dispatch my lover's replicant. I kicked the fat bastard for good measure as I left.

Chapter 34

Running through the corridors was complicated by more support beams and fixtures falling from above. Every several steps a change in the artificial gravity caused us and the surrounding debris to get suspended and then dropped.

McCord was having as much difficulty making progress as me. Though I wasn't sure McCord was the one driving the avatar. I realized earlier in the cells that the man was a clone.

"So who are you? Nate, Lucas, Tinker?"

"It's me this time—McCord," he said. "Nate will be in the shuttle soon. He's getting another avatar on-line to get the shuttle ready."

"What do you mean another Avatar online? There's no time to get another shuttle up here."

McCord laughed through his panting as we ran. "There are

plenty of his cloned avatars on the station. It wasn't just missiles and nano-tech in that shipment the Envoy brought."

"They stole Nate's design?"

"More like rerouted his shipment of a replicant fabrication device. Who do you think was making them for Nate?"

"And how long have you been playing puppet master to your own body double?" I asked McCord.

McCord told me that Nate had an avatar made for him years before. He admitted that the idea came up in idle conversation, but it was McCord who actually pushed for the avatars. McCord knew Nate's fascination with the technology behind the replicants and would go full steam into their creation.

"The first model was a bit clunky and robotic, but eventually the kinks were worked out. Those models also didn't have smooth and instinctual movement or waste management systems. I nearly ripped my pecker off with the first attempt at urinating."

The conversation as we headed out was a mix of joking at McCord's blundering first avatar to how we would handle Pincer. I suggested an outright assassination, while McCord wanted a more subtle approach.

"I think subtle went out the airlock when Pincer threatened to implant me with the centibot thing," I said. "I am really feeling the need to turn him over to the Resistance."

Our progress toward the shuttle dock was stopped when a jolt accompanying another loss of gravity stopped McCord. A beam that hovered above him came slamming down, severing one of his artificial legs.

"Well that is a problem," McCord said.

"Why, just leave the body. It's just an avatar."

"One of us needs to blow the shit out of this station. It can't be allowed to enter the atmosphere intact."

"So I'll go. Where are explosives stored?"

McCord's borrowed face smirked at me. "I am the explosives. My avatar is filled with the chemicals and compounds to make a sizable hole in the side of this station. If I'm by the reactor…bye-bye Space Force Space Station 2120."

McCord pulled a laser pistol from a dead soldier nearby.

"Put that sword to use and cauterize my leg after I heat blast the end of the blade."

I moved the sword near the pistol, allowing McCord to heat the end until the blade began to glow. The heat rose to the pummel, burning my hands. As I lifted the sword, bearing the sizzling pain that now baked the skin on my hands, I moved it to the end of what remained of McCord's severed limb.

McCord never flinched as I sealed the leg, stopping the flow of fluids from his body.

"Didn't even tickle," he said at my astonished gaze. "You can turn off the senses in these things, quite handy when being tortured."

"Now you tell me," I said. "What made Nate think of adding that feature?"

"You remember my first attempt at pissing? Now imagine feeling everything your avatar does including ripping one's own dick off."

"Got it."

I looked around us to find something to assist McCord as a crutch. Finding a frame from the ceiling tiles, I applied some leverage and bending with the sword. I fashioned a make-shift crutch, and I handed McCord.

"Now you get yourself to the docks, and I'll get to the reactor," McCord ordered.

"You need help."

"I'll be fine."

"You plan on hopping all the way like some deranged explosive rabbit?"

"You remember rabbits?" McCord asked.

"Yes I had one for a pet," I said. "Cute little thing."

"And tasty."

"Go, you monster," I said, looking at my bloody hand now staunched after holding the hot sword. "See you on the other side, hopefully."

McCord gave me a knowing nod and using the piece of debris from the walls as a crutch, made a break for the reactor room.

I grabbed the sword and headed off down the opposite corridor. The way was littered with wreckage and more than a few bodies. Once I made my way to the docking bay, I saw another Nate avatar on the opposite side.

Nate waved me on and hurried to the far side of my transport to the door. I hurried as best I could, being forced to backtrack and go the opposite direction when faced with a sizable hole separating me from my destination. Once I ran the opposite side, I came to the front of the transport and could see through the front viewport. I saw a silhouette from the light of the side door and felt a lift in my heart knowing Nate—or at least an avatar of him—was waiting for me.

As I came around the side, I saw Nate, but he wasn't alone. Holding a gun to his head was Pincer.

"I don't know if this one is the real one or isn't, but I'm not above finding out."

Pincer waved me forward with his weapon.

"Seems my own transport was disabled by a fallen support. Yours is ready to go."

"So why are you still here then, Pincer. Is it too menial a task to fly yourself?"

"On the contrary, I am rather good at flying. This Grunt-class vehicle of yours has a genetic lock that prevents me from initiating the engines it seems. A bit high-tech for such a low-brow as yourself."

I made my slow approach toward them, trying to determine what—if anything—I could do to disarm the Vice Chancellor. I could have allowed him to just shoot the Nate avatar, but something told me I might need him. I began chastising myself for dragging this damn sword along instead of the laser pistol. I was no knight, and this was not Excalibur. At least I didn't think it was.

"You have little choice here Elite wannabe. I have your little faggot boyfriend, and you have the means of starting the engines on this heap. So let's make a deal. The fruit for a finger."

Before I could say anything, Nate sent his head backward into Pincer's face. The cracking sound let me know that contact was made with Pincer's nose. The screaming man falling into a fetal position told me Pincer felt it along with every kick and punch Nate landed on him.

"Ok Nate, ease off," I said and pulled Nate off of the Vice Chancellor. "I think you proved your point."

"The fuck I did. A fruit is a rare piece of food these days thanks to you and your lot. I am not a fruit you shriveled dick, pussy-grabbing, hate-monger."

I let him get in a few more good kicks before forcing myself between them. I looked down at Pincer.

"Hate never wins you know," I said.

"You are a fool," Pincer said as I dragged him off my ship. "We are the Omega, in the end, it will be us alone."

"Then what? Without anyone to do all your work, clean up after you, feed you, pamper you. Your lot could not last without those of us who have to do everything for you."

"We will survive, we have been at this far too long, and nothing you can do can stop us." He spat at me. "That is the blood of purity."

Good to know, I thought. "You see this symbol on my lapel. The Omega-Cross pin of office I took from the Protectorate?"

"What of it, just proof you rely on the status provided by our good graces."

I turned the pin upside down. "You have no idea that it is a symbol of resistance. You may be represented by the Omega, here at the top, but what you don't see is the sword that is driven through your center."

I raised the sword I carried in both hands high above my head and drove it down through the center of pincer's chest. As he spat up the last of his 'pure' and real blood. I leaned over him.

"That will always be your weakness. Hate blinds you from seeing what is staring you in the face."

I took Nate into my arms and kissed him hard and let go of the sword. We walked into the shuttle, and as I turned for one last glance, I saw the name of the sword etched on the side for the first time. It wasn't Excalibur, it was called 'Aequitas'. The ancient Latin concept of justice, fairness, and equality.

Chapter 35

Getting off the station required heavy use of the firepower in my shuttle. We had to blast our way out the docking bay doors. Once outside the station, we witnessed the explosive blast of light and moment of fire that escaped the central rotation rigging.

McCord made it to the reactor and self-destructed. It was not the only signs of an explosion. From the corner of my vision, I caught a glimpse of blasts coming from the New Republic. All along the Mississippi River, there was a trail of flashes and smoke. It seemed the destruction of the space station was the signal the Resistance was waiting for.

The shuttle spun sideways as the concussive wave and debris followed behind our escape. I managed to regain control of our trajectory and turned back in time to see a stream of flame and metal escape the blast. A missile survived the explosion and was heading toward a target.

"Shit. We have to stop that missile," I said.

I hit the boosters and sped toward the missile as it cleared the opposite side of the station's blast radius.

Flying back into the blast wave jarred my body as I fought with the controls. It was difficult to steady the craft as we were jostled in all directions. I managed to keep the worst of the debris from taking us out, but the shuttle was taking damage from all the pieces of the station. I adjusted the shields to full power and rerouted back shielding power to the front. I was not worried about what might hit us from behind. There was a field of debris and bodies between us and the missile.

I fired my laser weapons at the missile, hitting debris and making few hits on my target. The shots that made contact with the missile were little more than an annoyance to the flight systems on the device. Each blow was deflected by a shield, and the missile would correct its trajectory. I soon ran out of power to the laser system. I would have to reroute power from the shields but couldn't do that until I was close enough. No shielding at that moment would have been a quick death. There was still too much debris, yet I was gaining on the missile.

I had only ballistic firing left that helped move smaller objects out of our path, but the larger ones I had to swerve around. Maneuvering became that much more difficult the tighter space got as I neared the missile. More debris was forcing me to begin hitting larger objects with the ship.

The bumping and shaking of the flight caused something to fall free from below the console. I felt it hit my foot and looked down to find the hypo-spray I stole from the lab. Lucas managed to stow it after-all. I picked it up and placed it in my pocket.

My attention was returned to flying too late, and I only

managed to swerve enough not to take a direct hit. The chuck of metal hit one of my left engines, and I had to compensate. I was near enough to try firing ballistics. Still, the missile shields protected its flank.

"Who made those things with shields?" I said. "I'm out of firepower."

"Not exactly," Nate said. "You can always ram the damn thing with the shuttle."

I took a moment to think about it before half-joking saying, "I was growing sorta attached to this old bucket of bolts."

"I'll buy you a shiny new ship, my love. Now set course to ram this bastard into that missile. I'll prepare the escape pod. We need to get you and that sample of nano-bots in your body to the UN."

I knew there was little chance an auto-course would succeed. I needed to wait until the missile entered the ionosphere where the shields would be disrupted before running it down. While the projectile had active shields, there was no guarantee that ramming would destroy it. I had to pilot the shuttle myself.

I set the course, but only to set Nate at ease and distract him with the pod. Walking up behind him I reached into my pocket. As he turned around, I took him in my arms.

"Really, you horny beast," he said. "This is hardly the time for that." Then he looked into the pod. "However, we could join the 300 mile-high club."

"A worthy goal," I said but changed the subject. I showed Nate my cauterized hand. "I know what you did." Then pointed to my missing scar. "I really wish you would have asked my permission."

"You would have said no."

"Likely, and admittedly would have been a fool to do so, but it would have been my decision."

"When did you find out?" Nate asked.

"I have always sensed something was odd. The missing scar, the ringing in my ears, the feeling I'd get passing through into space—it all never sat well with me. Even when you insisted I not use an avatar when leaving your lab, it didn't fully click. But then when I saw the blood from my hand, and that of the other avatars everything fell into place."

"You couldn't use an avatar, as an avatar already."

"Yes," I said before releasing the hypo-spray contents into Nate's avatar. "And I cannot succeed in stopping that missile without staying here, so you have to deliver these sample nano-bots."

The shock to his system temporarily incapacitated Nate. I dragged his spasming body along the floor, fighting against the bumping and jarring of the shuttle's flight. The shaking of Nate's avatar settled, and its systems were resetting, allowing me to place him in the escape pod.

"Mac, this is never going to work. Just get in the pod and let's get out of here."

"Now who is attached? This is just an avatar. I'll see you when this is done I expect I'm somewhere hidden in your lab?"

"Yes, I had your control tube and body moved in my lab while we were in flight there with Lucas and Tinker."

Nate tried to convince me to join him, but I had to see this through. Regardless of the missile's target, nobody deserved what having those nano-bots inside would do. And we needed the samples delivered intact for when the Omega tried again.

I smiled at Nate after kissing him goodbye. "You can add a shiny new avatar to that list of things to buy me."

"I might have a spare just laying around," Nate said and smirked.

"I love you, ya pervert!" I closed the pod and ejected it from the shuttle.

A proximity alarm sounded, and I ran to my piloting seat. I was approaching the ionosphere, and the missile was closer than expected.

I had to slow my approach if this plan was going to work. I needed to time everything to the second. If I hit the injectors at the wrong moment, I would overshoot and miss my target. I wouldn't get a second chance.

Everything hitched on the atmospheric boosters that allowed hypersonic speeds. Energy reserves were critical, and I didn't have enough available power for this one attempt. That meant I had to disengage the inertial dampeners and the shielding to make sure I managed enough power. I also had to add another source of energy. My avatar's battery.

I had no tools, so I used my lapel pin to slice open my abdomen. Remembering Nate's talk about the avatars, I stuck my hand into my gut and fished around until I found the power unit. I pulled it out enough to expose the mechanics and rest it just outside the jagged incision.

I needed something to connect the battery to the auxiliary power port. Looking around there was nothing, I even pulled a few panels to find only fiber optics, nothing wire. I slammed my hand on the console, and looked down to find my pinky held the answer.

The ring I bought from the street vendor weeks earlier slid easily off my finger. Unwinding the wire I fastened one end on the coil of my power supply.

"Now would be a good time to turn off the sense of touch in this avatar, because this is gonna hurt."

The last thing I needed now was a short circuit so I turned off all systems and safeguards except the engines. I looked at the power port with my hand hovering an inch away. Hesitating and holding my unneeded breath I waited a moment before shoving the wire in.

Working through the shock and drain to my system, I punched the booster injection button.

Fifteen seconds to impact. The ship moaned and creaked its displeasure under the unshielded stress. The noise became so overwhelming my own hearing gave up, or I just blocked out everything but the pain in my chest and eyes.

Ten seconds to impact. The pressure was blinding as my eyes filled with bright spots and all the air from my lungs was squeezed from my body. But the aching was leaving me along with the power in my battery.

Five seconds to impact. All the fluids from my body began to excrete from anywhere there was an opening. I would have laughed at the thought of shitting and pissing myself, but I had no power left.

Blackness.

Chapter 36

I always thought there would be light before the darkness, but it was the other way round. The blackness that enveloped me at that final instant before impact ended with painful light.

Every part of my body ached, especially my eyes when I forced them open. I tried to sit up and fell back from the spinning that filled my head.

"Easy there handsome," a smooth and familiar voice said. "You've been playing remote control man for longer than even I have."

Nate smiled down at me. I sniffed hard to pull in his spice and vanilla smell. I smiled back. I tried to reach for his head to pull him in for a kiss but missed.

"Don't get too frisky with this avatar pal. You'll have to wait for the real me when you arrive."

"Arrive where?" I asked and finally managed to sit up. "Why is everything all wibbly-wobbly? Am I broken?"

Lucas laughed and smacked my leg. "Nope. We're on a cruise ship out on the ocean."

"Hardly a cruiser, Lucas," Nate said. "Just one of my yachts. We couldn't stay in the New Republic once the wall started coming down. And the Protectorate became notified of your...status. We got things rolling, it's up to the people to finish reclaiming their rights and freedoms."

Nate told me of what happened nearly two weeks earlier after I ended one life, that of my avatar.

After the Station blew to pieces. Those fragments lit the skies with a showering call for revolution. I remembered the flashes of light from looking down at Earth. Nate confirmed that was indeed the first attack from the Resistance. The Great Wall was blown to pieces in many places from the Northern Border to the Gulf.

Once news of the fate of the space station broke, there was little controlling of the Grunts. The media tried saying the station disaster was espionage and perpetrated by enemies of the New Republic. The story changed several times before the press stopped talking about it.

The broadcasts were soon enough replaced with reports of civil unrest. Without being advised of what 'not' to report, there was a constant stream of news about riots, and the retreat of Enforcers from the Wall. The disturbances were not reported as a revolt by the General Population until a news station was taken over by Resistance agents. Among those now broadcasting was Scarlett.

She took to the role of press agent as though born to the post. She began reshaping the flow of information and funneling truth to the people.

Recordings from the past, including those of what really

happened during the Unifying Event, drew more members into the alliance between the Resistance and the UN. Canada and Mexico began supplying our fighters with medical supplies and food. The United Nations was not yet prepared to provide manpower, but that would change after the next few days.

Then the entire broadcast system was soon hijacked and began playing the full story. This was all thanks to Tinker and Nate.

Every moment of my life played out in the body of my avatar was recorded. Nate provided Tinker with the access and data to reconstruct everything that I was witness to while in the avatar. Those recordings were being played out on every screen in the New Republic and beyond.

The entire world had proof of the truth they suspected all along. And with the news of Lord Dampnut's and Pincer's demise, the fight to retake leadership of the New Republic and decide its fate was well underway.

"I wouldn't be too congratulatory just yet Mac," Nate said. "They have my plans and code for the avatars, remember. They also have the nanotech. The Omega are not going to just give up, but we have time since they don't do anything without formulating plans within plans."

"Well it certainly does not look good for the Omega," I said. "We could just start hunting them down, except that we don't know who they are."

"We have some leads, but let's not focus on tomorrow's problem." Nate moved Lucas out of his way. "Today we get you fixed up and ready for me in Argentina."

"Argentina? Why are we heading to the United Nations?"

If I hadn't already had a headache, the news Nate shared would have given me one.

First was that with the unrest in the New Republic, it was not a good place for me to be seen just yet. The Protectorate still had control of major cities and the Capitol. With a price on my head, Nate didn't have enough avatars available of me for my use.

Though the Resistance was entirely in support of me and still felt I was their leader, there were others who were out for my head beside the Protectorate. Not only the Elite who didn't already have an international business would lose their standing, wealth, power, and more, all the Enforcers and merchants that were not sympathizers were already looking for me.

The Enforcers were the brutal right hand of the Protectorate and the first targets for many in the Resistance and those who merely rioted from released oppression and anger. Hate was turned back on those who spread it, and it did not wear on them well.

Old Union President Penny Seloni was eager to take on the task of reunifying the country. However, with the rumors of her Envoy being involved in backdoor dealing and unsanctioned trade with the New Republic, The United Nations was not ready to back her.

As the Resistance moved to take the Capitol, they were calling for me to come and take over. The United Nations thought it best that we select representation from the Resistance in these early days, while I go to the UN and represent the reformation movement that the rest of the international community supported. I was trading one shit job for another.

I shook my head at the thought and looked around seeing who was missing. There was Lucas, looking at me like a lost puppy. Tinker was not there, nor was McCord.

Nate saw me looking about. "Tinker is leading the charge on the demolition of the rest of the Wall and appropriation of more technology for the Resistance. McCord has taken to hunting down Eli Minsk. That is after reuniting with the real Pornia. They're an item you probably guessed."

"Yes I was informed and realized the Pornia on the station was an avatar when Pincer attacked her," I said. "And where has Minsk gone?"

Minsk disappeared sometime before the station was destroyed. Nate had a brief communication with him that was described by Lucas as loud and full of new colorful adjectives. Once the truth of his duplicity was released to the Old Union, he was gone.

"Probably holed up in some remote tropical location with plenty of loose women and illicit drugs."

"Maybe he'll just disappear then."

"Not likely. He loves wealth and power too much. He does have good intentions from time to time, but ultimately he is no different from the rest of the Omega and Elite."

"Yourself not included," Lucas jibed.

"Go away you little shit starter," Nate said. "I admit to my lavishness and arrogance-"

"And spoiled," I teased.

I received a welcome smile. "And that...but I have never seen others as less than."

I smiled back and looked down at Lucas.

"And you...what are you going to do."

"I'm sticking with you, Mr. Mac. You're the closest thing to family I got. And you seem to be the safest dude to be around in a scrape."

I patted his shoulder. "Kinda like a big brother then?"

"More like great-great-great-"

"Alright you little shit," I interrupted. "I get it."

Lucas snorted as he headed up on deck. I heard the continued 'great-great-great-grandpa' fade as the ocean breeze carried his voice away.

When I was finally rested enough to walk, I looked around at the cargo of avatars and technology that was salvaged from Nate's compound in Miami. There was at least one of everything we would need to begin our pursuit of the Omega, but as Nate said, 'tomorrow's problem'.

I made my way toward a large window that showed a sunset over the coastal lands of Mexico. It would be a few days before we got to our destination, but it would be a beautiful trip. Seeing the world recovering from the devastation was welcome.

Destruction was wrought over a century and a half ago by a spoiled child wearing a man-suit. A man that ignorance allowed to take office and spread his hate, nearly destroying the planet.

I looked at my reflection in the glass of the window. I ran my finger over the scar that was prominent above my temple.

Today we celebrate this victory over hate, we celebrate the love of all kinds and embrace what makes us all different.

Today we've taken our collective heads out of our asses and begun thinking for ourselves.

Today we show those who dare tell us we are less than...that we are more and we are coming for you.

Tomorrow—Nate buys me that new shuttle.

CPSIA information can be obtained
at www.ICGtesting.com
Printed in the USA
FFHW021505180319
51110844-56572FF